"Are you sure you want to know the truth?"

He feared Kate Landon didn't have any idea what she was getting into. Worse, how dangerous it might get.

"I've always wanted to know the truth."

That feeling that he was meant to come here, meant to meet this woman, overwhelmed him. The answer *was* in this town, but so was the danger.

He was worried about her and not just because of his damn dream. She was putting her faith in him.

And he feared that if he kissed her, it wouldn't stop there.

He couldn't make Kate Landon any promises, and she was the kind of girl who deserved promises from a man.

USA TODAY Bestselling Author

B.J. DANIELS

BOOTS AND BULLETS

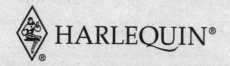

HARLEQUIN®

TORONTO • NEW YORK • LONDON
AMSTERDAM • PARIS • SYDNEY • HAMBURG
STOCKHOLM • ATHENS • TOKYO • MILAN • MADRID
PRAGUE • WARSAW • BUDAPEST • AUCKLAND

This book is dedicated to the Malta Quilt Club and all the other
wonderful and amazingly talented women who are teaching me
to have fun with fabric. Quilting keeps me sane
when words fail me. Thanks, ladies!

Recycling programs
for this product may
not exist in your area.

ISBN-13: 978-0-373-74555-5

BOOTS AND BULLETS

Copyright © 2010 by Barbara Heinlein

This edition published by arrangement with Harlequin Books S.A.

For questions and comments about the quality of this book please
contact us at Customer_eCare@Harlequin.ca.

www.eHarlequin.com

Printed in U.S.A.

ABOUT THE AUTHOR

B.J. Daniels wrote her first book after a career as an award-winning newspaper journalist and author of thirty-seven published short stories. That first book, *Odd Man Out*, received a four-and-a-half-star review from *RT Book Reviews* and went on to be nominated for Best Intrigue for that year. Since then she has won numerous awards, including a career achievement award for romantic suspense and many nominations and awards for best book.

Daniels lives in Montana with her husband, Parker, and two springer spaniels, Spot and Jem. To contact her, write to B.J. Daniels, P.O. Box 1173, Malta, MT 59538 or e-mail her at bjdaniels@mtintouch.net. Check out her Web site at www.bjdaniels.com.

Books by B.J. Daniels

HARLEQUIN INTRIGUE
996—SECRET OF DEADMAN'S COULEE†
1002—THE NEW DEPUTY IN TOWN†
1024—THE MYSTERY MAN OF WHITEHORSE†
1030—CLASSIFIED CHRISTMAS†
1053—MATCHMAKING WITH A MISSION†
1059—SECOND CHANCE COWBOY†
1083—MONTANA ROYALTY†
1125—SHOTGUN BRIDE*
1131—HUNTING DOWN THE HORSEMAN*
1137—BIG SKY DYNASTY*
1155—SMOKIN' SIX-SHOOTER*
1161—ONE HOT FORTY-FIVE*
1198—GUN-SHY BRIDE**
1204—HITCHED!**
1210—TWELVE-GAUGE GUARDIAN**
1234—BOOTS AND BULLETS††

†Whitehorse, Montana
*Whitehorse, Montana: The Corbetts
**Whitehorse, Montana: Winchester Ranch
††Whitehorse, Montana: Winchester Ranch Reloaded

CAST OF CHARACTERS

Cyrus Winchester—The cowboy private investigator woke from a three-month coma with a story about a murdered woman he'd seen in the hospital nursery who needed his help. Was it possible it had only been a bad dream?

Kate Landon—The owner of Second Hand Kate's was used to dealing with furnishings from the past. But it was her own past that haunted her until she met the P.I.

Roberta Warren—The hospital administrator swore there hadn't been a murder at her hospital while Cyrus had been in a coma there.

McCall Winchester—The sheriff didn't believe her cousin Cyrus's story had been more than a bad dream, either, until his questions stirred up a past some thought long forgotten.

Marie Dennison—She was dying, unaware of the storm that was brewing around something that had happened thirty years before on the night she gave birth.

Joanna McCormick—The ranch woman had every reason to hate the woman who'd tried to steal her husband.

Virginia Winchester—No one knew what had made her so bitter. But the truth was about to come out and she suspected her mother was at the heart of it.

Pepper Winchester—The matriarch had proven she was capable of almost anything. But even she couldn't be so heartless that she'd betray her own daughter, could she?

Candace Porter—Only two people in Whitehorse knew who she really was or what she was up to.

Katherine and Elizabeth Landon—They understood the bond between sisters right to the very end.

Chapter One

Cyrus Winchester opened his eyes and blinked in confusion. He appeared to be in a hospital room. From down the hall came the sound of a television advertisement for an end-of-season fall sale.

He told himself he must be dreaming. The last thing he remembered was heading to Montana to spend the Fourth of July with the grandmother he hadn't seen in twenty-seven years.

Glancing toward the window, he saw a gap in the drapes. His heart began to pound. The leaves were gone off the trees and several inches of fresh snow covered the ground.

A nurse entered the room, but she didn't look in his direction as she went over to the window and opened the curtains. He closed his eyes again, blinded by the brightness.

As he tried to make sense of this, Cyrus could hear her moving around the room. She came over to the bed, tucking and straightening, humming to herself a tune he didn't recognize. She smelled of citrus, a light, sweet scent that reminded him of summer and driving to Montana with the windows down on his pickup, the radio blaring.

With a start, he realized that wasn't the last thing he remembered!

His hand shot out, grabbing the nurse's wrist. She screamed, drawing back in surprise, eyes widening in shock. What was wrong with her?

He opened his mouth, his lips working, but nothing came out.

"Don't try to talk," she said and pushed the call button with her free hand. "The doctor will be glad to see that you're back with us, cowboy."

Back with us?

Cyrus tried again to speak, desperate to tell her what he remembered, but the only sound that came out was a *shh*.

The nurse gently removed her wrist from his grasp to pour him a glass of water. "Here, drink a little of this."

Gratefully he took the cup from her and raised his head enough to take a sip. He couldn't believe how weak he felt or how confused he was. But one thought remained clear and that was what he urgently needed to tell someone.

He took another swallow of water, feeling as if he hadn't had a drink in months.

"Sheriff." The word came out in a hoarse whisper. "Get. The. Sheriff. I saw it. The nurse. Murdered. In the hospital nursery."

Chapter Two

Cyrus tried to make sense of what his twin brother was telling him. "No, Cordell," he said when his brother finished. "I know what I saw last night."

His brother's earlier relief at seeing him awake had now turned to concern. "Cyrus, you've been in a coma for three months. You just woke up. You wouldn't have seen a murder unless it happened in the last twenty minutes."

"I'm telling you. I saw her. A nurse or a nurse's aide, I don't know, she was wearing a uniform and she was lying on the floor with a bloody scalpel next to her just inside the nursery door." He saw his brother frown. "What?"

"You're in a special rehabilitation center in Denver and have been for the last two months. There is no nursery here."

Cyrus lay back against the pillows, looking past his identical twin to the snow covering the landscape outside. "The hospital was a brick building. Old. The tiles on the floor were worn." Out of the corner of his eye, he caught his brother's surprised expression. "There is such a place, isn't there?"

"You just described the old hospital in White-horse, Montana, but you haven't been there for months," Cordell said.

"But I was there, right?"

"Yes, for only one night. They were in the process of moving you to the new hospital the night you were…"

"You're eventually going to have to tell me what happened to me," Cyrus said.

"What's important is that you're conscious. The doctor said everything looks good and there is no reason you shouldn't have a full recovery. As for this other issue, we can sort it out later when—"

"A nurse was *murdered*." Cyrus swallowed, his mouth and throat still dry from lack of use.

"I'm sorry, but it had to have been a dream. You say you got up out of bed that night—"

"I buzzed for the nurse, but no one answered the call button, so I got up and walked out past the nurse's station," Cyrus said, seeing it as clearly as his brother standing before him. "The nurses' station was empty, but I remember looking at the clock. It was two minutes past midnight. I could hear someone down the hall talking in whispers in one of the rooms. I walked in that direction, but as I passed the nursery windows—"

"Cyrus, this is the first time since your accident that you've been conscious," Cordell said gently. "That night in the old Whitehorse hospital, you were hooked up to monitors and IVs. There is no way you got up and walked anywhere. I'm sorry. I know it seemed real to you, whatever you think you saw, but it had to have just been a bad dream."

"Then how do you explain the fact that I can remember exactly how the old tiles felt on my bare feet or the way the place smelled, or that I can describe the hospital to you if I was never awake to see it?"

Cordell shook his head. "I don't know."

"Then you can't be certain that I didn't see exactly what I said I did."

"All I know is that if you had gotten out of bed that night in the old hospital, the alarms on the monitors would have gone off."

"Maybe they did. There were no nurses around to hear them. I'm telling you the place was a morgue and there was no one at the nurses' station."

"Even if that was true, monitors were recording your vital signs. If you disconnected anything and walked down the hall there would be a report of it."

"Maybe there is. Have you seen the records?"

His brother sighed. "You were moved to the new hospital the next morning. Don't you think someone would have noticed you were no longer connected to the IV or monitors?"

"Maybe the nurses covered it up because they were down the hall killing a woman."

"Cyrus—"

"I know what I saw," he said with a shake of his head. What frustrated him even more than not getting anyone to believe him was that after all this time, any evidence of the crime would be gone.

"I'm glad you're the same old Cyrus, stubborn as ever," Cordell said with affection.

"Were there any other patients in the hospital the one night I spent there?" Cyrus asked as a thought occurred to him.

"One of the reasons the ambulance took you to the old hospital was because there was another patient who couldn't be moved, so the hospital was still staffed for the night."

Sure it was. "Another patient? Maybe that patient saw or heard something that would corroborate my story."

"That patient was in his eighties. He died that night."

Cyrus sighed and closed his eyes.

"Listen, the doctor said you shouldn't overdo."

"I want you to call the hospital up there and the sheriff," Cyrus said, opening his eyes. "I'm telling you I saw a murder." He gave his brother a detailed description of the female victim.

"Okay, I'll check into it if it will make you take it easy for a while."

Cyrus lay back against the pillows on the hospital bed, exhausted. How was that possible after sleeping for almost three months?

"Get some rest," Cordell said, clasping his hand. "I can't tell you how good it is to have you back."

"Yeah, same here." He was glad one of the first faces he'd seen after waking had been his twin's. But he couldn't help feeling helpless and frustrated.

He'd seen a murdered woman that night in the hospital and no one believed him. Not even his brother.

CYRUS WOKE to find his twin beside his bed. Through the open curtains he could see that it was dark outside. How long had he been asleep this time?

Cordell stirred and sat up, seeing that he'd awakened. "How are you feeling?"

"Okay." Had he expected Cyrus to wake up and recant his story about the murdered woman he'd seen? Surely his twin knew him better than that. "What did you find out?"

From Cordell's expression, he'd been hoping, at least. "I called the hospital in Whitehorse and talked to the administrator. She assured me there was no murder at the old hospital the night you were a patient there."

"Someone moved the body."

"She also assured me that you never left your bed. There were two nurses on duty that night monitoring not only you, but also the elderly gentleman in a room down the hall. One nurse was just outside your room the whole time."

Cyrus knew that wasn't true, but Cordell didn't give him a chance to argue the point.

"I also called the Whitehorse sheriff's department and talked to our cousin McCall, who has since become the sheriff. There was no murder at the old hospital that night. Nor any missing nurse because both nurses who were on duty that night are accounted for. Nor was there a nurse's aide or orderly or anyone else working that night."

Then she must have just been dressed in a uniform for some reason, Cyrus thought.

"There was also no missing person report on any woman in the area."

She must not have been from Whitehorse.

He saw his brother's expression and knew that Cordell would have thought of all of this and asked the sheriff to run a check in a broader area with the description Cyrus had supplied. He and Cordell were private investigators and identical twins. They could finish each other's sentences. Of course Cordell would have thought of all these things.

"Sheriff McCall Winchester assured me that no unexplained vehicles were found near the old hospital nor has anyone in the area gone missing."

Was it possible everyone was right and that he'd only seen the murdered woman in a coma-induced nightmare?

Cyrus didn't believe that. But then again, he also couldn't believe he'd been in coma for three months.

WITHIN A FEW WEEKS, Cyrus was feeling more like his old self. He'd been working out, getting his strength back and was now restless. He hadn't been able to shake the images from the dream. In fact, they seemed stronger than they had the morning he'd awakened in the rehabilitation center.

He still had no memory, though, of what had happened to him in Whitehorse in the hours before the accident that put him in the coma.

Cordell had filled him in, finally. Apparently, he'd driven to Whitehorse in his pickup and stopped that night at the Whitehorse Hotel, an old four-story antique on the edge of town. He'd gone there, he remembered, to see his grandmother Pepper Winchester after receiving a letter from her lawyer giving him the impression that she might be dying.

Even now he couldn't remember why he'd wanted to go see the reclusive grandmother who'd kicked her family off the ranch twenty-seven years ago, never to be heard from again—until now.

In Whitehorse, he'd taken a room on the fourth floor of the hotel, intending to wait until his brother joined him the next morning before going out to the Winchester Ranch.

Apparently he had barely gotten into his room when he'd either heard something outside or happened to look out the window. What he'd seen, Cordell said, was a child molester breaking the only yard light in the hotel parking lot and slashing the rear tire of a VW bug parked there.

Cyrus must have watched as the man went back to the dark-colored van, the engine running, and realized the man was waiting for the owner of the VW to come out.

He'd run downstairs in time to keep the young woman who owned the VW bug from being run down by the van and killed. While saving her, he'd been hit and suffered a blow to his head that had left him in a coma all these months.

"That's some story," Cyrus said after his brother finished.

It was like hearing a story about someone he didn't know. None of it brought back a single memory. But it did fit in with his dream, since he'd spent a night in the old hospital.

During the weeks he'd spent getting stronger, he hadn't brought up the so-called murder dream with Cordell because it upset him. Cyrus suspected he worried about his twin's mental health. During his last checkup, even the doctor had questioned Cyrus about headaches, strange dreams and hallucinations. Clearly Cordell had talked to the doctor about his brother's inability to let this go.

"I didn't think coma patients dreamed," Cyrus had said to the doctor.

"Actually, they retain non-cognitive function and normal sleep patterns. It's their higher brain functions they lose, other than key functions such as breathing and circulation. You were in a deep-level coma caused by trauma to the brain.

I'm sure that explains what you thought you saw."

After his doctor's appointment, Cyrus stopped by Winchester Investigations, unable to put it off any longer. With each passing day, he had more questions—and more suspicions. He knew there was only one way to put his mind at ease.

"Hey," he said after tapping at his brother's open office door.

Cordell looked up and from his expression, he'd been expecting this.

"I have to go back to Whitehorse and check out a few things myself."

"I'll go with you."

"No, you need to stay here and do some work. We both can't be goofing off. When I come back—"

"Yeah, I want to talk to you about that."

"Is there a problem?"

"No, it's just that, well, you've met Raine," Cordell said.

Cyrus smiled. He'd been pleased when his brother had introduced him to the woman he'd been seeing for the last three months. Raine Chandler, he'd been surprised to hear, was the woman he'd saved up in Montana.

"So I brought you two together." Cyrus had never believed in divine intervention. But as eerie as this was, he felt as if it had all happened for a reason. And that reason, he feared, was so he could be at the hospital that night and make sure justice was done.

But that surprise was nothing compared to realizing his brother had fallen head-over-heels in love with the woman. After Cordell's horrible marriage and divorce, no one had expected him ever to consider marriage again—especially his twin.

But when he'd met Raine, he'd seen that she was wearing a gorgeous diamond engagement ring and Cordell was always grinning when he was around her.

"Raine and I made a deal back in Montana," Cordell was saying. He looked uncomfortable. "She said she'd marry me only when you could be my best man."

Cyrus was surprised. "She was taking one hell of a chance I was going to come out of my coma."

"Raine has a lot of faith. I think she knew how much I would need you at my side on my wedding day."

Cyrus laughed. "True enough. Congrats, Cordell, and I'd love to be your best man. So when is the big day?"

"We haven't set it yet. We were waiting to see…"

If Cyrus really was going to be all right.

That was the problem with being twins: sometimes you knew exactly what the other one was thinking.

"I'm fine, really. This is just something I need to do. I'm not crazy, no screws loose from the head injury. If you had seen what I did, you'd be doing the same thing. It was that real, Cordell."

His brother nodded. "So go to Montana, do what you have to do and—"

"Set a wedding date. I'll be there for you. This thing in Montana won't take that long, unless you're thinking of getting married right away."

"No, we were considering a New Year's wedding. Did I mention that our cousin McCall is getting married at the ranch at Christmas?" Cordell asked.

"You aren't seriously considering—"

"Raine and Grandmother hit it off." Cordell shrugged. "Grandmother thinks we should move our investigative business to Montana. I know," he said quickly, putting up a hand. "I told her you'd never go for that."

Cyrus had to laugh. Cordell was the one who had wanted nothing to do with his grandmother. He'd tried to talk Cyrus out of even going to Montana in the first place. Now he was actually considering another wedding at the ranch after Christmas?

"Hey," he said, "whatever you and Raine decide. Count me in." He hugged his brother and headed for the door.

"Call me when you get there and keep in touch," his brother called after him. "If you need me, I'll be there in a heartbeat. Or if I don't hear from you."

Cyrus stopped at the door to look back at him and laughed. "Stop worrying about me. I'll probably be back within the week. By the way, thanks for taking care of my pickup."

"Sure."

Cyrus got the feeling there was something his brother wasn't telling him. "You didn't let your girlfriend drive my pickup, did you?"

"The way Raine drives? Are you kidding?"

He started to step out into the hallway.

"Cyrus!"

Turning, he looked back at his brother and saw more than worry on Cordell's face. "Be careful."

Cyrus felt that bad feeling he'd awakened with rise to the surface again. If the murder had been nothing more than a bad dream, then why did his brother look scared for him?

Chapter Three

His first morning in Whitehorse, Montana, Cyrus headed straight for the new hospital. The squat, single-level building sat on the east end of the small western town. There was an empty field behind it, the Larb Hills in the distance.

For a moment, he stood outside, hoping the cool October day would sharpen his senses. He felt off balance, confused and a little afraid that the blow to his head had done more damage than anyone suspected—and all because of what he believed he'd seen that night in the old hospital.

The doctor had said he might have some memory lapses, either short- or long-term. He'd been warned that he might not feel like himself for a while.

"There are things you might never get back."

Like my sanity?

When he'd reached town last night, he'd

returned to the Whitehorse Hotel on the edge of town and taken the same room he had planned to stay in more than three months earlier.

He hadn't slept well and when his brother had called and he'd told him where he was, Cordell threatened to come to Montana. Cyrus had talked him out of it, assuring him he wasn't losing it.

Now, as Cyrus stepped into the new hospital's reception area, he wasn't so sure. Maybe he was wrong. Who saw a murder that never happened?

It wasn't just that no one believed him. They all made it sound as if it would have been impossible for anything he said to have actually happened. All of them couldn't be wrong, could they?

Of course, his first thought was conspiracy. But did he believe that even his cousin was in on it?

The hospital was smaller than most, but then Whitehorse wasn't exactly booming. Like a lot of small Montana towns, its population was dropping each year as young people moved away for college and better-paying jobs.

"May I help you?" The receptionist was in her early twenties with straight blond hair and a recently applied sheen of lip gloss. He stared at her name tag, not registering her name as he suddenly had a flash of his so-called murder dream. The woman lying dead in the nursery hadn't been wearing a name tag. So maybe he was right and she wasn't a nurse. Or maybe she'd lost her name tag in the struggle.

"Sir?"

Cyrus stirred, blinking the receptionist back into focus. He removed his Stetson. "I need to speak with your hospital administrator." He realized he should have made an appointment. Had he been afraid the person wouldn't see him once he recognized the name and knew what this was about?

"Your name?"

"Cyrus Winchester."

The receptionist picked up the phone. "Let me see…oh, here she is now."

A woman in her sixties with short gray hair walked toward them. She was dressed in a suit and had an air of authority about her.

"This man needs to see you," the receptionist said.

The hospital administrator gave him only a brief glance. "Why don't you come back to my office."

Cyrus followed her into a small, brightly lit room. The light hurt his eyes. Another side effect of the coma, this sensitivity to light?

"Would you like me to close the blinds?" She

was already closing them, dimming the room a little.

"I'm Cyrus Winchester."

"What can I do for you, Mr. Winchester?" She didn't introduce herself but the plaque on her desk read *Roberta Warren.*

"Were you also the administrator at the old hospital?" he asked.

"Yes. I've been the administrator for the last thirty-four years." She clasped her hands together on her desk and seemed to wait patiently, although her demeanor said she had a lot to do and little time.

He kneaded the brim of his hat in his lap, surprised he was nervous. "You know who I am."

"Yes."

"Then you probably know why I'm here." He realized he was nervous because he was sitting in front of a health care specialist who was looking at him as if he might be nuts.

"Your brother called us about an incident you thought you'd seen while at the old hospital the night you were there."

"That *incident* was a woman murdered in the nursery."

She shook her head. "There was no murder at the hospital."

Another chunk of memory fell as if from the

sky. "There were two babies in bassinets," he said as he saw the nursery clearly in his memory. Why hadn't he recalled that earlier? Because it hadn't registered? Or because it hadn't mattered when there was a dead woman lying just inside the nursery?

Now, though, he thought the fact that the two babies were there did matter for some reason. He tried to remember, but that only made his head ache and the memory slip farther away from him.

Roberta Warren was still shaking her head. "There were no babies in the nursery that last night the old hospital was still open. I'm afraid you're mistaken about that, as well."

He tried another tactic. "Do you know a woman with long auburn hair, greenish-blue eyes, tall, slim, maybe in her late twenties or early thirties?"

"As I told your brother, there is no one employed at the hospital who matches that description."

"Do you know anyone in town who matches that description?"

She raised a brow. "I thought you said it was a nurse who you thought you saw murdered."

"She wasn't wearing a name tag when I found her. Maybe she was only pretending to be a nurse."

The administrator looked at her watch pointedly. "I'm sure you've spoken with the sheriff. Had there been a murder—"

"I'd like to speak to the two nurses on duty that night," he said.

"I won't allow that."

"Why not?" he asked, thinking he might be on to something.

"I've questioned both of them at length, Mr. Winchester. One was always at the desk that night. The sheriff also questioned them as well and looked at the monitor readings. You never left your bed that night. If you decide to pursue this, it will have to be with a subpoena and just cause." Her tone said *good luck getting either.* "I won't have you accusing my nurses of something that never happened."

He rose to his feet. He wasn't going to get anything from this woman. "Thank you for your time."

She sighed and gave him a sympathetic look. "I'm sure your doctor explained to you that what you thought you experienced was a coma-induced hallucination of some kind, perhaps stemming from your line of work. There is no cover-up, no murder, no reason for you to waste your time or anyone else's. I would think you would be glad to be alive and have better things to do with your time."

"I am glad to be alive. Unfortunately, the woman I saw lying in a pool of blood in the old hospital nursery isn't and for some reason no one cares."

He saw that his words finally hit home because she had paled. But that gave him little satisfaction. He turned and walked out of her office and reception area into the bright October morning.

He was shaking inside. Where had that come from about the babies? But now that he thought about it, he was certain there'd been two babies in the nursery.

Just as he was certain there'd been a murder. Now all he had to do was prove it—against all odds, because his instincts told him he was right. If that woman was ever going to get justice, it would be up to him.

THE MOMENT the office door closed, Roberta Warren let out the breath she'd been holding. Her hands were trembling as she reached into the drawer for the small bottle of vodka she kept there disguised in a water bottle.

Taking a sip, she told herself that there was no reason she should be so upset. But when Cordell Winchester had called questioning whether or not there had been a murder more than three months ago at the hospital, she hadn't thought anything of it.

That was because he hadn't mentioned that the murder his brother thought he'd seen had been in the hospital nursery. Or that the woman had been found in a pool of her own blood. Or that there had been two babies in bassinets in the nursery the night of the murder.

Roberta Warren took another sip of the vodka and quickly put the lid back on the water bottle. Her hands were a little steadier, but her heart was still pounding. The man couldn't have possibly dreamed any of this. Who dreamed a murder in such detail? But was he just fishing or did he know something?

She took a mint from her drawer and chewed it, debating how to handle this. The best thing was to ignore it. Cyrus Winchester would tire soon since he would keep running into dead ends, and he would eventually go back to Denver.

But then again, she hadn't expected him to come all the way to Whitehorse to chase a nightmare. She'd heard the determination in his voice. The fool really thought he was going to get justice for the dead woman.

Calmer, Roberta picked up the phone and almost dialed the number she hadn't called in thirty years. She put the phone down. She was overreacting. That was probably what he hoped she would do. But still she worried that this would get all over town, hell, all over the county, if he continued to ask questions.

If he didn't give up soon, she would have to come up with a way to dissuade him.

She stood, smoothed her hands over her skirt and walked to the window, half expecting to see Cyrus Winchester standing outside her office, staring in as if he thought he could make her feel guilty enough to panic.

Well, he didn't know her, she thought, but she was glad to see him drive off anyway.

THE OCTOBER DAY WAS sunny and blustery. Golden leaves showered down from the trees and formed piles in the gutters. The air smelled of fall with just a hint of the snowy winter days that weren't far off.

He was driving down a wide, tree-lined street when he saw the single-level brick building. Even with the sign removed, Cyrus recognized the old hospital. The realization gave him a chill.

As he pulled to the curb, he saw that apparently the movers hadn't completed the job of removing the furnishings, because there was a large panel truck parked out front and both front doors of the building were propped open.

Getting out of his pickup, Cyrus walked along the sidewalk past the truck. The back was open, a ramp leading into the cavernous, dark interior. He glanced in and saw a dozen old wooden chairs, some equally old end tables and several library tables.

As he passed, he saw that on the side of the truck were painted the words *Second Hand Kate's*. Under that in smaller print, *Used Furnishings Emporium*.

"Hello?" he called as he stepped through the open front doors of the old hospital. The interior still had that familiar clinical smell and that empty, cold feeling he remembered. He reminded himself that it had been empty now for more than three months.

"Hello?"

No answer.

He walked down the hallway, his boot heels echoing on the discolored worn tile. He hadn't realized where he was going until he reached the nursery windows.

His breath caught in his throat as he shoved back his Stetson and, cupping his hands, looked through the blank glass. The cribs and furnishings were gone, the room bare, but he could see it as the nursery had been in his memory.

A half dozen bassinets, but only two babies.

Both boys with little blue blankets and ribbons on the bassinets, he recalled with surprise.

He touched his fingers to the pane, then quickly pulled them away as a memory moved through him like a spasm. With a jolt, he remembered seeing the murdered woman right *before* she was killed.

He had stood in this very spot and watched her switch the babies in the bassinets.

"CYRUS, DO YOU REALIZE what you're saying?"

He'd had to go outside to get cell phone service.

"I saw her purposely switch the babies. Cordell, she stood there for a long moment as if making up her mind."

He could almost hear his twin's disbelief.

"I know how crazy it sounds, but when I saw this place as I was driving by, even without the sign, I knew it was the old hospital because I recognized it. Cordell, I walked straight to the nursery. When I touched the glass—" He shuddered at the memory. "I felt something so strong, I can't explain it."

"Okay, let's say you saw this woman who was later murdered after switching the babies," his brother said finally. "It should be easy enough to find out if there were two baby boys in the nursery while you were there."

He sighed. "I already asked the hospital administrator. She swears there were no babies in the nursery that night."

"So you think she's lying? The whole town is lying? Why would they do that?"

Cyrus had no idea. He was more concerned with how he was going to prove it. "The hospital administrator won't let me talk to the nurses who were on duty that night without a subpoena." He heard his brother sigh. "I have to go see the room I was in. I'll call you later. Stop worrying about me. I know what I'm doing."

He disconnected and walked back into the hospital. He felt scared as he entered the long corridor of worn tile. He'd heard the fear in his twin's voice. Maybe he couldn't trust his own judgment. Or maybe it was just that no one else trusted it.

Cyrus heard someone singing from one of the maze-like hallways deep in the building. At least that was real, he thought. The woman had a good voice and he recognized the country-western song. It was one of his favorites.

Past the nursery, he walked down to what he was certain had been his room. It was right beside what had been the nurses' station. Didn't this prove that he had regained consciousness at some point while still in this hospital that night?

He started to step into the room when he saw her. She came out of a doorway at the end of the hall and started toward him, a pair of iPod buds in her ears. She was singing along with the song, completely lost in the music.

As she came closer, Cyrus felt all the air rush out of him.

It was her!

The woman he'd seen switch the babies in the hospital nursery. The woman he'd found murdered right here in this old hospital more than three months ago.

Chapter Four

Cyrus stared at the woman as if she were an apparition. Everyone was right. He *was* losing his mind. Fear turned his skin clammy. He told himself he was seeing things, imagining her the same way he had the murdered woman.

As the young woman looked up then and saw him, she appeared startled. She slowed, looked unsure. He half expected her to vanish before his eyes.

"Can I help you?" she asked, frowning, as she walked toward him. Was it possible she recognized him? Or was she just surprised, thinking she was alone in the building?

As she drew closer, he saw that either his memory was in error or this wasn't the woman. But she looked enough like the murder victim to be her sister. Her hair was more copper than auburn, her eyes emerald rather than aquamarine and she was shorter than the murdered woman, although about the same age.

She had a small wooden nightstand in one hand and a slat-back wooden chair in the other and she wore blue denim overalls over a white T-shirt, sneakers on her feet. The logo on the overalls read *Second Hand Kate*.

"Are you all right?" she asked as she plucked out the earbuds.

He knew he must have lost all color. While he'd been getting stronger every day, the shock of seeing her had left him feeling weak and shaky.

He realized how bad he must look when she asked, "You know the hospital moved, right? Do you need someone to drive you up to the new one?"

He could hear the murmur of the music coming from the iPod in her overalls pocket. He shook his head and finally found his voice. "Sorry, I called out as I came in…"

She smiled. It seemed to light up the old building and the sweet innocence in the gesture tugged at his heart. This wasn't the woman he'd seen murdered in the nursery, but she had to be a relative. Wasn't it possible she'd seen him at the hospital?

"Do you know me?" he asked.

She looked at him as if he might be joking. "Should I?"

He shoved back his Stetson and smiled

sheepishly. "You look familiar. I thought… You don't happen to have a sister, do you?"

"Sorry." She was smiling again as if she thought this was a bad pick-up line.

She was definitely not the woman he'd seen. This woman, while the spitting image of the murder victim, lacked the darkness he'd felt in the dead woman. This woman was all sunshine and rainbows.

"Is this for the secondhand shop?" he asked, motioning to the furniture and then to the logo on her overalls, desperately needing to say something that didn't come out stupid.

She nodded, clearly pleased with the items. "They don't make furniture like this anymore. I can't wait to refinish some of these pieces," she said, her enthusiasm bubbling out.

"So you must be Kate." Not a nurse. Or even a nurse's aide here at the hospital.

"The Kate in Second Hand Kate's." She set down the chair and wiped her free hand on her overalls and held it out to him. "You aren't interested in used furniture, are you?"

"I might be," he said, realizing he was flirting with her. He held out his hand. "Cyrus Winchester."

"*Winchester?* You're not related to—"

"The sheriff is my cousin and Pepper is my grandmother."

"Oh." She chuckled. "I see."

"You know them?" he asked.

She shook her head. "I just moved here, but I've heard stories. Your grandmother is pretty famous around here. I've always wanted to meet her."

"Infamous, you mean." The Winchesters had always provided fodder for good gossip. His grandmother had been a recluse for the past twenty-seven years, his grandfather had ridden off on a horse one day forty years ago and never been seen again—until recently—and one of his uncles had only turned up after a gully washer had washed up his remains.

She turned her smile on him again. "Kate Landon."

Cyrus felt a gentle shock run through him at her warm, strong touch.

"So you just happened to stop by the hospital to…"

"Return to the scene of the crime." She laughed and he added quickly, "So to speak. I was brought in a few months ago by ambulance and spent a night here. I don't remember much about it. They tell me I was in a coma."

She instantly sobered. "Oh, I'm so sorry."

"I'm fine now." *Sure you are. You thought this woman had been murdered just down the hall in the nursery. Or at least her sister had.*

Except she doesn't have a sister. "I'm just going to take a look around, if that's okay."

"Sure. Just do me a favor, if you don't mind. This is my last load. Close the doors when you leave? There's a chain with a padlock on the outside that loops through the door handles."

He'd forgotten how trusting people were in small towns. "I'd be happy to lock it on my way out."

"Thanks." She seemed to hesitate, her green eyes darkening. "Take care of yourself."

Cyrus knew he was being paranoid, but her words seemed to echo in the still, empty hallway like an omen.

KATE CARRIED the end table and chair out to the truck, put it in the back with the last of the furniture, pushed in the ramp and slammed the rear doors, smiling to herself.

It had been a while since a man had openly flirted with her—let alone a very handsome cowboy. At the memory of the man she'd met inside, her gaze felt pulled back to the old hospital. The interior was deep in shadow, but she thought for a moment she saw movement in the darkness behind the open double doors.

Her friend Jasmine, a Whitehorse native, had kidded her about watching out for ghosts at the hospital. "Seriously, the nurses used to tell stories of feeling something in that old hospital when they worked the night shift and this one nurse swore she saw the ghost of this woman coming down the hall toward her."

Kate had laughed, figuring Jasmine was just fooling with her. She'd felt a little creepy in the old building alone earlier, but had just turned up her music. Now though, she would have sworn she saw a figure just beyond the doorway.

But when she'd turned to look down the long side of the building, she'd seen a set of white metal blinds flash open at a window in a far room.

Cyrus Winchester peered out for a moment, then closed the blinds again.

She felt a chill, remembering the feeling that someone had been watching her from just inside the hospital doors. It couldn't have been Cyrus. Had someone else been in there?

"It's the ghost of that woman," Jasmine would have said.

Fortunately Jasmine wasn't with her.

You're just imagining things. But she decided she would swing by later and make sure no one had gotten locked inside the old building.

As she climbed behind the wheel of her truck, she forgot all about ghosts. It was Cyrus Winchester she couldn't get off her mind. He had startled her earlier when she'd looked up and seen him standing in the hallway. Blame Jasmine for her darned ghost stories.

Cyrus Winchester had looked nothing like the legendary ghost woman standing there so tall, dark and exceedingly handsome.

Yet there had been something haunting in his eyes…

She shivered at the thought, remembering that when he'd seen her he'd looked as if he was the one who'd seen the ghost. Probably just recovering from his injuries. Still, it was odd, him wanting to return to the scene of the crime, as he'd said. Who visited his old hospital room?

She looked again at the windows where he'd peered out just minutes ago. With the blinds closed, she could see nothing but white metal.

Turning the key, she started the engine and a Christmas song came on the radio. It was too early to be thinking about Christmas. She was still gearing up for her annual Halloween haunted house. She turned the radio dial until she found country and western and turned her thoughts to Halloween.

She planned to transform the basement of Second Hand Kate's into a haunted house. She'd only been in town for a few months and it was her way of welcoming the community into her new store. The basement of the old two-story, once-a-library building with all its nooks and crannies was the perfect place for chills and thrills.

Fortunately, she'd managed to make a couple of friends who'd offered to help her. Jasmine was sewing some of the costumes and backdrops while Andi preferred working with the blood and guts, turning perfectly normal food into something gross and frightening.

Kate couldn't wait to hear the children's shrieks and screams, giggles and gags. She hoped for a good turnout Halloween night. But she still had a lot of work to do and was glad she'd finally gotten the last of the furniture out of the old hospital. There had been no hurry, but she hated leaving anything undone.

As she drove away, her cell phone rang.

"I found the most perfect fabric for the ghost in the pit of horror," Jasmine said, making her laugh.

"Of course you did. I was just thinking of you." She'd met Jasmine soon after she'd come to town at where else? A garage sale. The two had realized how much they had in common when they'd both tried to buy the same ugly chair.

"Oh, yeah?"

"I was just leaving the old hospital with the last of the furniture."

"You saw the ghost." Jasmine sounded excited. "Didn't I tell you?"

"What I saw was no ghost. I just ran into Cyrus Winchester."

"Who?"

"Pepper Winchester's grandson. You've never met him?"

"No. So what is he like?"

"Gorgeous." She almost added, "and a little strange," but chastised herself for even thinking it. The man had just come out of a coma.

"Sounds like a Winchester. Black hair and eyes?"

"Uh-huh. Tall with broad shoulders and slim hips that look great in Wrangler jeans." Kate remembered how good-looking he'd been standing there in his Stetson and boots. Even now she couldn't put her finger on what it was about him that had left her feeling afraid for him.

"Wait a minute, is he the one who was in the hospital with the coma?" Jasmine and Andi always knew more of what was going on than Kate ever did. Jasmine worked at City Hall so she heard all the good stuff and Andi was the local newspaper reporter.

"Uh-huh."

"He and his brother are private investigators in Denver. I heard he's *drop-dead* gorgeous and that he and his brother are identical twins," Jasmine said.

"Really?" She felt a chill at discovering Cyrus was a private investigator, but tried to hide her reaction from her friend. She'd never told anyone in Whitehorse about her past.

"What was he doing at the old hospital?" Andi asked.

"He stopped by to visit his room."

"Seriously? Don't you think that is a little macabre? Maybe he died there, you know, went toward the light but was pulled back and now he's trying to call up the other side."

"Or maybe you've been spending too much time planning the haunted house," Kate suggested.

Her friend laughed. "Swing by and I'll show you the fabric. I also have some old white curtains I can use for the ghosts, but I want your opinion first."

Kate was tired and dirty from hauling dusty old furniture, but she agreed. "See you in a minute." She hung up and on impulse, circled around the block and made a point of driving back past the hospital.

The pickup with the Colorado plates that had been parked behind her truck was still there, which meant Cyrus Winchester was still inside the hospital.

What *was* he doing in there?

THE HOSPITAL ROOM was exactly as he remembered it. Cyrus had quit asking himself how he knew that. Obviously he hadn't been unconscious the entire time.

When he'd opened the blinds, he'd seen Kate Landon sitting in her truck. Was she worried he wouldn't lock up? She couldn't be worried that he'd steal anything, since clearly there was nothing left in the building to steal.

He'd dropped the blinds and searched the room, not sure what he was hoping to find. Of course there was nothing either in the room or the bathroom but dust. How quickly the building was falling into disrepair.

When he peeked out the window again, the Second Hand Kate's truck was gone. He had wanted to question her further, but had warned himself not to ask too many questions that would scare her.

She looked too much like the murder victim not to have some connection. He would have to find out what he could about the Landon family.

Leaving his former hospital room, he walked down the hall, his boot heels echoing. The place had taken on an eerie feel. He stopped to listen as if he thought he could tap into the building's history, feel all the lives that had traveled through here from birth to death and all the broken bones and illnesses in between.

But of course he couldn't. He wasn't psychic. He'd seen someone switch two baby boys in the nursery and then become a murder victim. That was a far cry from being able to tell the future.

He thought about calling Cordell and telling him about Kate Landon. But he knew his brother would try to come up with some reason Kate looked so much like the murder victim.

"You must have seen her before you were attacked, before the coma, and unconsciously put her in your dream," Cordell would say.

Unfortunately, everything that had happened between his last memory of driving to Montana and waking up was lost. Except for what had happened that one night in the old hospital. He knew that alone should be proof the murder was just a bad dream.

At the nursery, he paused. It was just inside there that he'd found the dead woman. He walked a few feet down the hall, found the door into the nursery and stepped in.

Fortunately the power company hadn't turned off the electricity yet. He snapped on the light and studied the room, trying to picture where the bassinets and other equipment had been in this room that night.

At the back of his mind, a thought nagged at him. Why was the equipment still here that night? Why were there two babies still here if most everything had been moved to the new hospital?

He shoved the thought away. It didn't make any sense, but then again none of it did.

Cyrus moved to within feet of the spot where he believed the body had been sprawled. The woman had put up a struggle. In the semi-soundproof nursery and the near-empty hospital, it was no wonder no one had heard it.

Crouching down, he studied the worn tile. There were scuff marks, dust, some dirt and a scrape where something heavy had been dragged out. He wondered if the blood would show up in the thin cracks between the tiles with the luminol crime labs used?

Unfortunately, there was little chance of getting the crime lab involved, since the sheriff's department wasn't even investigating the murder.

Because there was no murder. No switching of babies in the nursery. No way you could have seen a dead woman because you were in a coma tethered to your bed by tubes and monitors. All this was just a coma-induced bad dream.

Sometimes he wished he had dreamed all of it so he could just quit this. As he started to push himself to his feet, he was blinded by another flash of memory. The woman lying in a pool of blood, him leaning over her, something on her wrist.

A string of tiny silver sleigh bells. A bracelet. One of the bells had come off and lay on its side in the blood next to her clutched fingers. The woman had put up a fight.

HEAD ACHING and even more mystified, Cyrus left the old hospital and drove down to the main drag. He parked in front of the *Milk River Examiner,* the local weekly newspaper, and climbed out, breathing in the crisp Montana air. The detailed images that kept flashing through his memory were starting to worry him.

Why hadn't he remembered all of it the moment he'd awakened? Why did it keep coming to him, little pieces that were so clear.… He shoved his worry away and entered the newspaper office.

It was small and sold paper supplies as well as putting out a weekly edition.

He took a current newspaper—and one from three months ago that would have come out the week he was taken to the hospital and the week after that. From the young clerk behind the counter, he also borrowed the phone book long enough to look up the last name Landon.

The nearby towns along the Hi-Line were all small enough that they'd been put into the same phone book. There was only one Landon in the entire the directory. Kate. What had he been thinking? If she had any female relatives here, they could be married and have different last names.

Returning the phone book to the clerk, he paid for his newspapers and stepped outside. Across the street was a small park next to the railroad tracks. He sat down at one of the picnic tables and opened the first newspaper.

The paper had a lot of local news about who was in town visiting and who had a birthday or anniversary. He paused on an ad for Second Hand Kate's, complete with an address and news about her recent opening—and her first annual haunted house to be held there Halloween night.

Cyrus realized Halloween was only a few days away.

There wasn't anything else in the paper that caught his eye, so he picked up one from three months ago. Under the sheriff's department reports he found the incident that had put him in a coma. It was brief, only a few words about a deputy responding to a call at the Whitehorse Hotel where a man had been attacked and taken to the hospital. The suspect was still at large.

He scanned through the rest of the four-page paper and found the obituary for the man who had died in the hospital the same night Cyrus was there. The man's name was Wally Ingram.

On impulse Cyrus called 411 on his cell and was put through to Wally Ingram's home number. He was surprised when it rang. He'd been half expecting to hear the line had been disconnected following the man's death.

"Hello?" The woman sounded young.

Cyrus quickly explained that he'd been in the hospital the same night as Mr. Ingram and wondered if any of the family had also been there.

"My mother stayed with Grandpa that night."

He felt his pulse quicken. "I'd like to talk to your mother if possible. Is she around?"

"Martha's gone to Great Falls and won't be back until late tonight, but you could probably catch her tomorrow morning."

He left a message to have Martha Ingram call him and hung up, feeling hopeful. Someone else had been in the hospital that night, someone not connected to the staff.

The answer was in this town, Cyrus thought, and felt a strange sense of apprehension. Little scared him, but he knew at the back of his mind, he was beginning to question his own sanity.

CYRUS CHECKED the newspaper from a week after his accident and read about his brother and another private investigator from California, Raine Chandler, catching some child molesters, one of them responsible for putting him in the hospital.

As he walked back to his car, he felt antsy. The air had cooled down some, the day not quite as beautiful as it had been. He wondered if a storm was coming in.

Sliding behind the wheel of his pickup, he didn't kid himself about where he was going or why as he drove down the street to the address that had been listed in the newspaper for Second Hand Kate's. He was relieved to see the Open sign in the window.

Getting out, he climbed the steps of the large, old brick building. Over the door, he could make out the faded letters of the word *Library*. She'd put her shop in an old library building.

The door opened, a bell tinkled and he caught the scent of orange and cinnamon. He breathed in the sweet, rich smell, glad of the warmth inside the shop as the door closed behind him.

He'd expected piles of old furniture—not this decorated, attractive shop.

"Be right with you!" Kate called from somewhere above him. He noticed a beautiful, wide stairway that climbed to the second floor. There was a small sign that read Private.

As he walked around the lower floor, he saw that each room had its own setting, each unique and charming. It felt almost magical, the lighting, the tapestries, the overstuffed chairs, the colors and textures, trinkets and curios. He remembered what she'd said about refinishing the furniture she'd gotten from the old hospital and could see her handiwork throughout her shop.

He could well imagine the condition many of the old items had been in before she'd worked her magic. It surprised him what wonders she'd achieved with a collection of what most people would have discarded as worthless. He could feel Kate's energy in every room. It was like walking into the woman's home rather than a shop.

At a rustling sound, he turned to see Kate Landon come down the wide flight of stairs. She'd showered and changed since he'd seen her at the old hospital and now wore a colorful skirt and top with black ballet slippers.

Her hair was still damp and hung around her shoulders, a coppery wave that framed her face and set off her wide green eyes. She was so stunning he stared, completely enchanted with this woman who could turn trash into treasure. As he stared at her, he realized that before, all he'd seen was her resemblance to the dead woman, now...

"Hello," she said in a lyrical tone. She seemed amused to see him again.

"After meeting you, I decided I'd better see your shop," he admitted honestly.

She smiled, opening her arms to take in the expansive rooms. "It's still a work in progress. I haven't been open all that long. I bought the building at an auction four months ago."

So she had been in town before his coma. Which meant he could have seen her, just as his brother would have suggested, and that was how she became part of his nightmare.

"Your shop is amazing. You've done wonders with it," he said glancing around although all he really wanted to do was look at her.

"Halloween night the basement is being turned into a haunted house," she said. "You should come. If you're still in town."

"I just might do that." His gaze locked with hers. "Do you have plans for dinner tonight?" The invitation came out of nowhere, surprising them both.

Her eyebrows shot up.

"I realize we just met and you know nothing about me."

She smiled. "In a town this size? Are you kidding? Everyone in town knows your life history by now."

He returned her smile. "I hope what you heard wasn't all bad."

"Not *all* of it," she teased. "I'd love to have dinner with you, but I'm afraid I have other plans tonight."

Of course she would have a date, a woman like this.

"I have to help my friend Jasmine sew some props for the haunted house. She sews, I help by providing the food and moral support. But I am planning on stopping by the Fall Festival later this evening. Maybe I'll see you there if you're going. There's going to be frybread. I never pass up frybread."

"Great." Cyrus wondered if this woman was why he was supposed to come back to Whitehorse. Maybe it hadn't been about a murder at all. Maybe he'd been destined to return to meet this woman. He liked the idea much better than the alternative.

It made more sense than any other explanation he could come up with. Which would mean there was no murdered woman in the nursery. No switching of babies. No wandering down an empty hospital hallway. None of that had happened.

Instead Kate Landon had happened. He

smiled to himself, desperately wanting to believe she was the reason he was in Whitehorse as he shoved off the doubts that had plagued him, the things that made no sense.

He told that nagging little voice demanding a logical explanation for everything to shut up. It didn't matter why he'd walked right to the old hospital nursery earlier today, why he'd been able to find his room, why he knew how the tile felt on his bare feet, or the big one, why Kate Landon looked so much like the murdered woman that he'd thought she was the victim's younger sister.

Couldn't it be possible that he'd had the dream just to get him back here to meet Kate?

Cyrus felt as if a weight had been lifted off his shoulders. He was freer than he'd felt since he'd awakened from his coma. He told himself that he could let it go.

Those months would always be lost, but he had come out of the coma with apparently no long-lasting side effects. He'd been lucky. He was alive. It was time he started enjoying that fact. Just as Roberta Warren, the hospital administrator, had told him.

But as he turned to leave, Cyrus saw something in a glass cabinet that changed everything.

Chapter Five

"Do you like the bracelet?" Kate asked as she joined him at the glass case.

For a moment, Cyrus couldn't find his voice. He told himself there had to be hundreds, thousands of bracelets just like this one. But even as he thought it, he could see that this wasn't costume jewelry.

"It looks old," he said as he stared down at the delicate string of tiny silver sleigh bells and tried to still his thundering heart. He saw that it had been made by a jeweler with an eye for detail. "It's incredible workmanship."

Kate beamed. "My grandfather was a silversmith. He made the bracelet for my mother's sixteenth birthday."

"Your mother?" he asked, his voice sounding strained to his ears.

When she didn't say anything, he said carefully, "There's no price on it."

She laughed softly. "Because it's *priceless,*"

she said as she unlocked the case and gingerly lifted out the bracelet. The bells tinkled softly, sending a chill through him. He'd heard that sound before. A memory, unfocused and distant, tried to surface.

"The items in this case aren't for sale. I just like them where I can see them," Kate said, pulling him out of the memory. "It makes me feel closer to my mother. I can't bring myself to wear the bracelet. I like that she was the last person to wear it. Silly, I know."

"No," he said, looking over at her and thinking he couldn't be more enchanted by this woman.

"It's really quite heavy," she said, surprising him as she laid the bracelet in his palm.

The silver felt cold against his flesh and sent a memory of another palm clutching this bracelet ripping through his mind. He quickly handed it back to her and started to ask more about her mother when the front door jangled open and three women came in with a gust of cold air. Wind whirled golden leaves around the steps before the door closed again.

"Good afternoon," Kate said with a smile as she greeted the shoppers. Cyrus watched her quickly put the bracelet back in the case and lock it. "Maybe I'll see you later at the Fall Festival," she whispered as she passed him to go offer the women a cup of hot spiced cider.

He stood for a moment, staring at the bracelet, before he noticed the women glancing back at him with obvious curiosity.

As he left his mind was awhirl.

The bracelet he'd seen in his dream was real. That had to mean that the woman wearing it had also been real—and murdered in the hospital nursery just like he'd known from the moment he'd awakened from his coma.

If the bracelet had belonged to Kate's mother, then she had to be the woman he'd seen in the nursery. The same woman who'd switched the babies.

WHEN THEY'D BEEN interrupted by the three local women entering the shop, Kate had felt as if Cyrus had wanted to ask her something more.

As she gave the women a tour, she was again struck with that uneasy feeling she'd had when she'd met Cyrus at the old hospital. He hadn't just stopped by her shop out of curiosity. He wanted something from her and she suspected it was more than a date.

As more women entered the shop, Kate replayed the moment when Cyrus had seen her mother's bracelet in the glass case by the door.

At first she'd thought he was taken with it. But now that she thought about it, he'd seemed shocked to see it, almost as if he'd recognized it.

Her heart began to beat a little faster. Was it possible he knew something about her mother?

Now she wished she didn't have to work on the haunted house tonight. She would make sure she saw Cyrus Winchester again. Unfortunately, she had no idea where he was staying or how to reach him. She would have to make a point of catching up with him at the festival tonight—if he went.

Kate thought he would go and be watching for her. Apparently he was as anxious to see her as she was him.

Another group came through the door, then a handful of singles. Kate was busy showing them around her shop when she heard the bell over the front door ring again. She turned, half expecting to see Cyrus coming back through the door because she'd been thinking about him.

But it was her friend Andi Blake Jackson.

"What is going on?" Andi asked as she stepped in out of the cold. Andi was the local reporter for the *Milk River Examiner,* the only newspaper for miles. She used to be a famous television newscaster in Texas, but she'd moved to Montana and fallen in love and as they say, the rest was history. Andi had become a permanent Whitehorse resident when she'd gotten hitched to Cade Jackson, who ran the local bait shop and raised horses on a place out by Nelson Reservoir. His family went way back in Whitehorse.

Kate and Andi had met when Andi did a story on Kate's purchase of the old library building and her plans to open Second Hand Kate's. They'd become fast friends.

"I was down the street and I couldn't help but notice people coming and going in the shop. I thought 'what is she selling?' And then I found out. You know why business has been so brisk, don't you?" She didn't give Kate a chance to guess. "Cyrus Winchester. The talk around town is that he stopped by your shop. Everyone is dying to know what he bought."

Kate had to smile. Andi had been born to be a reporter, with her natural curiosity and ability to ferret out news.

"Is that the man's name?" Kate asked, pretending to play dumb.

Andi cocked a brow at her suspiciously. "Give it up. Jasmine already told me that you met him at the old hospital earlier. What was he doing here?"

She shrugged. "I think he was just looking."

Looking for what, though? Cyrus's interest had been less in Second Hand Kate's and more in Kate herself. Had it not been for his interest in the bracelet, she would have been flattered at the attention. It had been a while since she'd taken an interest in anything but getting her business going. Cyrus Winchester interested her. Now more than ever.

"He didn't buy anything?"

"Nope." Kate stepped behind the counter to sort through some new stock she'd purchased at one of the last of the season's garage sales.

"Then why..."

Kate had shared only the basics of her past with her new friends in Whitehorse. There were some things she'd never told anyone. But she knew Andi and knew she would keep digging if she thought there was something going on. "Cyrus asked me out to dinner."

Andi narrowed her gaze. "Get out of here. You do know what he's doing in town, don't you? He's been asking a lot of questions about a murder."

Kate checked her expression before she looked up from her garage-sale finds. "Murder?"

"This is where it gets really weird," Andi said, looking around to make sure no one was within earshot. "There *wasn't* a murder. The night he spent in the old hospital he thinks he walked down to the nursery and found a nurse murdered there, but he couldn't have because he was in a coma the entire time and never left his bed."

"So he dreamed it?"

"He doesn't think so."

"How do you know this for a fact?" Kate demanded, not liking that this was what everyone in town was talking about.

"I have a source at the hospital," Andi whispered. "Her office is just outside the administrator's and she hears everything."

"So who did he think he saw murdered?" Kate asked, hating being part of the gossip and yet wanting to know more about Cyrus. Feeling as if she needed to know more about him and why he might be interested in her—and her mother's bracelet.

Andi shrugged. "All he said was that it was a nurse who worked at the hospital. And get this, he thinks there were two babies in the nursery that night."

"But there weren't any babies in the nursery."

Andi's eyes widened. "How do you know that?"

"Because I was there that night. Martha Ingram's father, Wally, was in the hospital and at her suggestion I stopped by to discuss buying some of the furnishings. You know she's on the hospital board. I think she thought talking about that would keep her mind off the fact that her father was dying."

"So did you see or hear anything?"

Kate shook her head.

"You didn't see Cyrus Winchester?"

"No. Martha and I talked out in the hallway. I saw the nurses behind the desk down the hall. Now that I think about it, I saw one of them go into the room next to the nurses' station to check on the only other patient." With a start she realized that had to have been Cyrus Winchester. "I just remember it was kind of weird with the hospital being so empty that night."

"Creepy," Andi said. "What if there really was a murder there that night?"

"I thought you said there wasn't?"

Andi shrugged. "Still, you have to admit, it's interesting that he is so determined there was a murder that he came all this way to check it out for himself. Clearly he's mistaken, since there was no murder victim found and no babies in the nursery that night."

Kate nodded, remembering the empty nursery she'd passed as she'd left that night three months before. Interesting? Or very odd? "I wonder why he's so convinced?"

"Maybe he's got a screw loose after being hit in the head or he just imagined it. You know he spent three months in a coma and only recently came out of it."

He was in a coma that long? Kate thought about how pale he'd looked when she'd seen him in the old hospital hallway earlier. He hadn't looked well. She was reminded that she'd thought then that he'd looked as if he'd seen a ghost.

"Well, I would imagine he will give up and go back to wherever he's from soon," she said.

"Denver. He's a private investigator in Denver with his twin brother, Cordell. They're the grandsons of Pepper Winchester, a recluse who lives on a ranch forty miles south of here. He's never been married."

Kate laughed, thinking now she really did have his life history. "You left out his shoe size and that he's quite handsome."

"You noticed? I thought you didn't have time for men?"

Andi had tried to set her up with several eligible bachelors when she'd first come to town, but Kate hadn't been interested. "So are you going out to dinner with him?"

"I'm busy tonight, but I might if he asks again." Kate realized that something had drawn her to Cyrus Winchester, something more than his good looks, as if they had some...connection—even before she'd seen his strange reaction to her mother's bracelet. As Andi had put it, creepy.

"I'm not sure you should go out with him," Andi said. "What if he *is* crazy? Jasmine said when you met him earlier at the old hospital he was looking for his room?"

"I was loading up the last of the furniture I bought at the auction. He said he wanted to see the room where he'd stayed that one night." But he hadn't been searching for his room. She got the feeling he'd gone straight to it.

"He came back to the scene of the crime?"

Kate realized that was probably exactly what he'd been doing. In fact, he'd said something to that effect. She shivered now at the memory.

Another group of women entered the shop on a fresh blast of cold air and autumn leaves. "I wonder if there ever have been any murders at the old hospital?" Kate whispered as the women disappeared into the back of the shop.

"None that I know of," Andi said, thoughtfully.

Kate knew her friend. If anyone could track it down, it was Andi. "Let me know what you find out."

A COUNTRY-WESTERN BAND played on a flatbed trailer parked along the main drag. Fall Festival was in full swing by the time Cyrus got there.

He hadn't seen Kate Landon, wasn't even sure she'd show up.

Seeing that silver bracelet in her shop had thrown him for a loop. Then when she'd told him it had belonged to her mother...

He'd gone back to his hotel room and spent most of the afternoon trying to make sense of it, as if any of this made any sense. Maybe seeing Kate and the bracelet was just a coincidence. Just like the murder had been nothing more than his overactive imagination at work.

His head hurt and he tried to put all of it out of his mind as he walked along the crowded streets clustered with booths offering everything from crafts and home-grown pumpkins to Christmas-tree ornaments and baked goods.

A mixture of alluring scents floated along the street: burgers, chocolate, coffee, hot apple cider, barbecue, cotton candy. But one scent in particular drew him until he found the booth where women were making frybread.

He breathed in the delicious aroma, remembering another fall when he was five and his father brought him and Cordell into town for the Fall Festival.

"Two?" the woman behind the counter asked.

Cyrus started. Did he look as if he needed two frybreads? That's when he noticed Kate had come up beside him and was doing the same thing he'd done, breathing in the wonderful aroma.

Her eyes were closed as she breathed in the scent of the frying bread, her expression one of unmitigated pleasure. He smiled to himself, guessing he'd had the same look on his face just moments before.

"Two," he confirmed as Kate Landon opened her beautiful green eyes. He couldn't believe how happy he was to see her and that happiness had nothing to do with his reason for coming to Whitehorse. "I take it you like frybread," he said with a grin.

"I *love* frybread. This is why I wasn't about to miss the Fall Festival or miss seeing you again." She seemed to blush as her last words came out. As he handed her one of the confections covered with sugar and cinnamon, she said, "Thank you, but you didn't have to buy mine."

"My pleasure," he said, taking his own and motioning to one of the picnic tables in the small park by the railroad line that still took passengers as far as Seattle or Chicago and all points beyond.

"How is the haunted house coming along?" Cyrus asked as he took a seat across from her.

"Slowly but surely. I've been so busy with getting all the furnishings out of the old hospital and opening my shop that I'm behind." She took a bite of her frybread, emitting a soft satisfying groan.

He watched her, smiling as she licked the sugar and cinnamon from her lips, making it hard for him to concentrate on the questions he wanted to ask her.

"So are you a Whitehorse native?"

She opened her eyes and shook her head. "West Yellowstone."

"That's quite a change, from a tourist town surrounded by mountains to a prairie town on the Hi-Line just miles from Canada. How did you end up here?" he asked. It was an odd place for a single woman to open a business—unless she came with a husband or a lover, or had family here, he thought.

She chewed for a moment. "You know how some people spin the globe, close their eyes and pick a spot at random?"

He nodded. "I understand that's how a lot of towns along the Hi-Line got their names—Malta, Zurich, Glasgow."

"Well, it wasn't quite that impulsive, but close."

"So you don't have any family here?"

"I didn't know a soul when I arrived four months ago, but people are friendly here and I've settled in fairly well."

"You must like it if you started a business."

"Now *that* was impulsive," she admitted with a laugh. "I just happened to hit town during an auction. As you might guess, I'm a sucker for auctions and garage sales. When I saw that old library building was being auctioned off, it was love at first sight and the price was dirt cheap. Of course it needs work.…" She shrugged, her cheeks dimpling as she smiled.

He thought she couldn't look cuter with a few grains of sugar and cinnamon at the corner of her mouth, her emerald eyes sparkling and that smile on her lips.

"How about you? Other than visiting your former hospital room, what brings you to White-horse?" she asked.

He realized she'd just been waiting for her turn to ask him questions. He figured she hadn't been kidding earlier about knowing his life history and wondered what in particular she wanted to know. "Originally, it was because of my grandmother. She'd been a recluse for twenty-seven years so I haven't seen her since I was seven. I got a letter from her lawyer, saying she wanted to see me and the rest of her family." He shrugged. "Pepper Winchester is…well, there is no one like her. She'd make a great wicked witch for your haunted house."

Kate laughed, a wonderful, light sound that

made the night feel even more magical. "Was she really that bad when you saw her?"

"I haven't seen her yet. I got waylaid in June when I drove up to see her."

"The coma," Kate said, sobering. "What happened?"

He gave her an abbreviated version of what he'd been told by his brother and had read in the local paper. He got the feeling she might have already heard some of it. What he didn't tell her was that he now knew why his grandmother had asked him and the rest of the family to come back to Winchester Ranch.

It had to do with his uncle, Trace Winchester. Trace was the youngest son of Pepper and Call Winchester and Pepper's favorite. Just recently it was discovered that Trace was murdered twenty-seven years ago.

Before that he was believed to have taken off, running from a pregnant wife and a poaching charge.

Cyrus's grandmother, it seemed, believed that a member of the family might have been involved in Trace's murder. She was getting everyone back to the ranch to question them.

She particularly wanted to question her grandsons after discovering they might have witnessed something from a third-floor room at the ranch—a forbidden room that had once been used as punishment.

"It sounds like trouble has a way of finding you," she said, studying him. "My instincts tell me to give you a wide berth. Tell me I'm wrong about that."

"I'd listen to your instincts," Cyrus said, sounding and looking serious.

Kate wished she could. But her instincts also told her that this man knew something about her mother.

Not just that. She'd noticed when he told about how he'd ended up in a coma, that he'd left out the part about how he'd saved Raine Chandler's life.

After helping Jasmine finish the ghost costumes, Kate had made a point of reading the article about Cyrus her friend Andi had been kind enough to print out for her. She'd remembered most of the articles about the child molesters from several months ago, but hadn't put the names together.

Cyrus had almost lost his life. As it was he'd lost three months. The man was a hero, an honor she saw he didn't wear comfortably.

Was that why she feared—even though the odds were against it—that he really had seen a murder at the hospital? But how could that have anything to do with her mother or her bracelet?

She finished her frybread, wiped her fingers on the napkin and dabbed at her mouth. She knew she was taking time to screw up her courage and it wasn't like her. She thought of herself as being fearless—at least most of the time.

"I need you to tell me why you reacted the way you did earlier when you saw my mother's bracelet," she said bluntly.

Just as she'd expected, she caught him flat-footed. He didn't seem to know what to say.

"I know you think you saw a murder at the old hospital the night you were a patient there," she continued quickly. She'd heard concern in his voice, and when she looked into his dark eyes now she saw worry for her there. There was a connection, just as she'd feared.

"It has something to do with me, doesn't it?" she said. "That's why you looked as if you'd seen a ghost when you saw me at the old hospital, why you came by the shop and why you were so upset when you saw my mother's silver bracelet."

He stared at her in surprise and maybe a little awe and she knew she'd connected the dots correctly. Her heart hammered in her chest. She'd hoped he'd ask her what the devil she was talking about. Or at least try to convince her she had gotten it all wrong.

"Are you sure you want to hear about it?" he asked quietly.

Her pulse thundered in her ears at the gravity in his voice. "Yes." She'd gotten this far in life by meeting obstacles head-on. She couldn't stop now. Taking a breath, she asked the one question she feared the most. "Does this have something to do with my mother?"

"Why would you think what I have to tell you might involve your mother?"

She shook her head. As far back as she could remember, she'd had a feeling that her mother hadn't died the way her grandmother had told her.

"I have my reasons," she said.

He just looked at her. She could tell he didn't want this to be about her mother any more than she did.

"Do you have a picture of her?" he asked finally.

"Back at the shop." As she pushed to her feet, her legs felt weak as water. After all these years, was she finally going to find out what really had happened to her mother? Or was it just as her grandmother had told her and everything else was nothing but a child's overactive imagination?

She hated questioning the stories her grandmother had told. Would she be questioning her mother's death now if it wasn't for that postcard she'd found in her grandmother's jewelry box?

ON THE WALK BACK, Cyrus asked about her mother and the bracelet.

"My grandmother told me she died of pneumonia just after I was born."

"You don't believe that?"

She shook her head, clearly not wanting to get into her reasons.

"What about your father?"

"He was in the military, killed before I was born in some training exercise that went wrong. They were to be married when he came home on leave. He didn't even know my mother was pregnant with me when he died."

She'd never known either of her parents? Cyrus thought about his own mother, who'd hung in with his father just long enough to give birth to her twin boys before she'd split. He'd never gone looking for her, though sometimes he thought about it.

"My grandmother, Dimple, raised me."

"Dimple?"

She laughed. "A nickname. She had these wonderful deep dimples when she smiled and she smiled a lot." Her own smile faded. "She passed away four months ago."

Four months. Right before Kate had come to Whitehorse.

"So Landon was your mother's name as well as yours." He could see that talking was taking her mind off the reason they were walking back to her shop.

"Yes."

Cyrus was as nervous as she was about seeing photographs of her mother. Kate's resemblance to the woman he'd seen murdered was too much of a coincidence, then throw in the bracelet... Still, he reminded himself that everyone in town swore there had never been a murder. But for his own sanity, he desperately needed to know why he'd dreamed all of this.

THEY HAD ALMOST REACHED Second Hand Kate's when Cyrus asked, "How old were you when your grandmother gave you your mother's bracelet?"

"She didn't." Kate still felt the betrayal. Why hadn't her grandmother given it to her? "I found the bracelet after my grandmother died. It was hidden in the back of her jewelry box." Along with the postcard.

"Hidden?"

"I don't think my grandmother could bear

seeing it." Or didn't want Kate to see it for some reason, she thought. Just like the hidden postcard.

They stopped at the bottom of the wide concrete stairs that led up to the front door of the shop. Suddenly Kate was afraid to go inside. All these years she'd told herself she wanted to know the truth. But did she? What if her mother had simply run off and her grandmother's story was only to protect her?

"I don't see what any of this has to do with the bracelet or my mother. She couldn't be the woman you saw in your dream. How would that be possible?"

"I'm sure you're right."

So why was she so frightened? She knew the reason. "The woman you saw in your dream resembled me, didn't she?"

"Yes."

She took that news like a blow even though she'd suspected as much given his reaction to her at the hospital. She looked into his handsome face and saw real concern for her. He was as scared as she was that somehow the murder he'd seen involved her.

"Let's get this over with." Kate pulled out her keys, her fingers trembling as she tried to get the key into the front-door lock.

Cyrus gently took the key ring from her and opened the door.

"Thank you." He handed the keys back. She stepped past him to turn on a light and heard him close and lock the door behind them. A car went by with a burst of teenagers' laughter. In the distance, Kate could hear the low hum of activity at the festival, but the deeper they moved into the old library building, the more deafening the quiet became.

"If you'll wait here, I'll go up and get the photograph album," she said and hurried up the stairs. She hadn't invited him up because she needed a moment to herself. At the top, she had to stop and catch her breath. The weight of what was about to happen sat like a boulder on her chest.

The album was where she'd put it in the hall closet. Taking it down carefully, she hugged it to her. These were the only photographs she had of her mother and like the bracelet, they were priceless to her.

When she felt a little steadier, she headed back downstairs. She told herself that Cyrus Winchester's dream couldn't possibly be about her mother. Because her mother hadn't been in Whitehorse three months ago. Because in her heart, she knew her mother was dead. But what scared her was that she also knew her mother hadn't died the way her grandmother had told her.

As she came down the stairs, she found him waiting where she'd left him. She motioned to a Victorian velvet couch and carried the album over to it to sit down.

Cyrus joined her. He looked as nervous as she felt as she opened the album to the photographs of her mother taken thirty years ago.

"This is Elizabeth, my mother." Carefully, she slid the album over to him and held her breath.

CYRUS GLANCED DOWN at the young woman in the snapshot. She was holding a baby in her arms and smiling at the camera. She had auburn hair and wide green eyes and her resemblance to Kate was disturbing—Elizabeth Landon had looked just like her at about the same age.

He could practically hear Kate holding her breath next to him. "She's not the woman I saw murdered."

Her breath came out on a sob. She stumbled to her feet and stood with her back to him for a moment. He thought about going to her, trying to offer her some comfort, but feared it would not be welcome. He was the one who'd put her through this pain. And for what?

Cyrus looked down at the photo album in his

lap, studying the woman and baby for a long moment before turning his attention to the other photographs.

He felt his heart drop to the pit of his stomach and must have made a sound because Kate turned to look at him.

"Who is this woman?" His voice sounded odd even to him.

Kate made a swipe at her tears as she looked from him to the album in his lap. His tone must have warned her because she stepped almost cautiously back to the couch and stood looking down at the open photo album.

"What woman?" she asked in a desolate voice.

"That one." He pointed to another young woman. In the photograph she sat in a corner chair holding a baby. Kate, he assumed. What was haunting was that her features were nearly identical to Elizabeth Landon's, but he had known at a glance that they were not the same woman.

Her hair wasn't auburn but bleached blond. The wide blue-green eyes were unmistakable, although there was a sadness in them as well as in her expression.

"That's Aunt Katherine, my mother's older sister," she said in barely a whisper. "I was named after her. People used to say they looked so much alike they could have been twins." Kate raised her gaze as she said it. She bit her lip, her eyes flooding with tears as she lowered herself to the couch. "Aunt Katherine is the woman you saw."

He hadn't had to answer. She'd seen his expression and was already shaking her head. "That's not possible. Katherine's been dead for thirty years. She died just before I was six months old. She'd always had a weak heart…"

Cyrus stared down at Aunt Katherine's photo, wondering what in the hell was going on. This was the woman he'd seen lying in a pool of blood in the old hospital nursery. This was the woman who'd switched the babies just moments before her death and what had weakened this woman's heart was the scalpel that had stabbed her in the chest.

Chapter Six

Kate couldn't catch her breath.

"Look, everyone keeps telling me it was just a bad dream and obviously it must be," Cyrus said. "I don't understand any of this, like why I dreamed about this woman or that bracelet or why when I saw you and realized how much you looked like…" His eyes widened in alarm as he seemed to realize how much distress she was in. "Kate, I'm so sorry. I—"

"Please," she managed to say as she stumbled to her feet again. "I need you to leave."

"Kate—"

"I just need to be alone."

He shot to his feet. "Of course. I'm sorry. I should never…" For a moment, he looked as if he might reach for her to try to comfort her.

She took a step back. She knew that if he took her in his arms she would break down completely.

"I'm staying at the Whitehorse Hotel, room

412. If you need to get hold of me just to talk or…"

Kate could see how sorry he was for upsetting her, but right now she couldn't deal with any of it. She felt as if her world was crumbling around her. She ushered him out, then stood with her back against the locked door, shaking so hard she had to hug herself to keep from falling apart.

She'd thought she wanted to know the truth. But she'd been so sure he would say he didn't recognize her mother. And he had. She'd been so relieved.

Until he'd asked about her aunt Katherine, the woman she'd been named for. She'd never dreamed the woman he'd thought he'd seen murdered would be her aunt.

All the doubts she'd had her whole life shot to the surface. Kate had lived on the stories her grandmother had told about her mother and her aunt. Even as a child, she'd known her grandmother had exaggerated many of the stories.

For some time now, she had suspected it had been more than Dimple just not being truthful with her.

If her grandmother had lied about the way Aunt Katherine died, then didn't it follow that she'd lied about Kate's mother's death, as well?

So what had really happened to them?

She quickly reminded herself that Cyrus Winchester's coma dream might be just that, nothing more than a weird nightmare. But like him, she was having a hard time believing that, given that he'd identified her aunt as the murder victim in his dream—a woman who'd been dead for almost as many years as Cyrus had been alive.

According to Cyrus, Katherine had been murdered in the Whitehorse hospital nursery. Kate thought of the postcard from her mother that she'd found hidden in her grandmother's jewelry box—and the postmark on it. The card had been dated thirty years ago this December—several years after her grandmother had sworn both daughters had died.

The postcard from her mother made it clear that both her aunt and mother had been in Whitehorse. Wasn't it possible that Cyrus Winchester's dream was the missing piece of the puzzle she'd been searching for?

Suddenly, Kate felt a chill. What if the reason no one believed Cyrus's story was because the murder hadn't happened three months ago—it had happened thirty years ago?

CYRUS MENTALLY KICKED himself as he'd stepped out into the cold fall evening air and heard Kate lock the shop door behind him. She was afraid of him, probably thought he was a psychopath or at the very least a sadist.

He should have realized that the only reason she'd shown him the photograph of her mother was that she wanted him to tell her the murdered woman wasn't her mother.

He'd been shocked when he'd recognized the aunt's photograph. That was definitely the woman he'd seen. But how was that possible? Kate said her aunt had died of a weak heart more than thirty years ago—she hadn't been murdered in the hospital after switching two baby boys in the nursery. What was wrong with him going to Kate with all this?

Because he'd hoped that she held the answers.

Now all he had was more questions. Still he was reeling from what she had told him. Both her mother and aunt had died thirty years ago when Kate was only a baby?

And neither had been murdered?

All he'd done was bring up bad memories for her. He wished to hell he'd never had the dream. But then he would never have met Kate. Yeah? Well, he should have just left it alone. Because Kate didn't want anything to do with him now. Not that he could blame her.

Cyrus drove to the Whitehorse Hotel and sat

for a while in his pickup, unable to face the desolate room, cursing himself and trying to make sense of all this. Since he'd awakened from his coma he hadn't thought about anything else. All it had done, though, was give him a headache.

He'd been so sure Kate was the reason he'd been drawn back to Whitehorse.

Now he didn't know what to think.

Shaking his head, he climbed out of the pickup behind the old brick hotel. He had no memory of this place, but it was here in this very poorly lit parking lot that he'd almost lost his life.

The night was cold and clear, trillions of stars flickering over his head and a moon as large and golden as any he'd ever seen. He stopped for a moment to find the Big Dipper, just as he had done as a kid, and then went inside to climb the stairs to his fourth-floor room.

What he hated the most was that he couldn't get the mess out of his mind. If Katherine Landon had died from a weak heart thirty years ago, then how could he have seen her lying in a pool of blood in the old hospital nursery? And what about the babies he swore he saw her switch? What had become of them—if they ever existed?

As much as he hated upsetting Kate, he still felt as if the damned dream was real and that

not only was the answer here in Whitehorse,
but Kate was the key.

KATE PACED THE FLOOR after Cyrus left, too
shaken to sit still. Her mind was racing. None of
this was true. It had just been a dream. Dreams
meant nothing.

So why was she so upset?

Because she hadn't told him everything.

She stopped pacing. Standing in the middle of
her shop, she tried to talk herself out of what she
was about to do, but it was useless. Retrieving
the envelope from the safe behind the counter,
she grabbed her jacket and purse, locked up the
shop and headed for her van.

Wisps of clouds drifted across the harvest
moon that seemed to hang over Whitehorse. An
omen? She laughed at that. She'd already seen
the future—and the past, she thought as she
parked behind the Whitehorse Hotel.

At room 412, she almost changed her mind.

Cyrus opened the door to her quiet knock.
He seemed surprised—and pleased—to see her
standing there and maybe a little wary. "Kate,"
was all he said as he held the door open.

She entered and heard him close the door
behind her. Out of habit and no doubt to keep
her mind off the real reason she was here, her
gaze went to the furnishings. A couple of pieces

in the room she wouldn't mind having for her shop—after she'd refinished them.

"I'm not sure why I came here," she said, turning to look at him.

"It doesn't matter, I'm just glad you're here. Would you like something to drink? I can get us a cold soda from down the hall."

"That sounds good." After he left, she walked to the window, glanced out at the darkness and told herself she had to be honest with him. She knew how hard it had been for him to tell her about his dream.

And more than ever she believed that they'd both ended up here in Whitehorse for a reason.

Kate turned as he came back. She took the icy-cold can of diet cola he handed her, glad to have something to do with her hands, and opened it to take a sip. It felt good going down. She met his gaze and was strengthened by the kind look on his face.

"I thought we should talk," she said.

Cyrus sat down on the edge of the bed, motioning for her to take the only chair in the room. It was a straight-back wooden chair much like the ones she'd purchased from the old hospital.

"The reason I got so upset earlier was that I've never understood why my mother would leave me when I was just a baby," she said after taking a seat. "The truth is I don't know what really happened to my mother or my aunt. But I know my mother didn't die of pneumonia. My grandmother—"

"Dimple."

Kate smiled. "Yes, Dimple. She used to tell me stories about my mother and aunt and what they were like growing up. I'm not sure anything she told me was the truth. I know my mother, Elizabeth Landon, left me when I was six months old. This I know from a postcard I found in my grandmother's jewelry box after her death. It was postmarked Whitehorse, Montana."

"That's why you came here," Cyrus said.

She nodded. "It was the last place I knew my mother had been. But once I got here, I couldn't find any evidence of that. Whitehorse was the end of the trail."

"In more ways than one," he said.

Kate nodded. "Not everyone appreciates Whitehorse. From the moment I arrived here, I just felt that the answer was in this town." She caught his change of expression. "You believe that, too, don't you?"

He did, but he wasn't ready to admit it. Any more than he was ready to admit that any of this made any sense at this point. "You don't know why your mother was in Whitehorse?"

She shook her head. "All the postcard said was that she was sorry she had to leave when she did and was grateful to my grandmother for taking good care of me and that she would be home soon. She said she was bringing my aunt Katherine home with her."

"You don't know if that was the last time your grandmother heard from her?"

"No. The date on the postcard was months after my grandmother said both my mother and aunt had died. I'd always thought it peculiar that my aunt and mother would die within weeks of each other. But Dimple said she thought it was because they had been so close and loved each other so much."

"You have reason to believe that isn't true?"

Kate knew what he was asking. Did she have reason other than just her intuition? "My grandmother saved everything. All her important papers, like my birth certificate, were in her safe-deposit box. There were no death certificates other than my grandfather's in the box."

Cyrus shook his head as if he wasn't sure what she was saying. "Maybe she never put them in the safe-deposit box at the bank."

"There are no death certificates for either my aunt or my mother. She made up the stories because she didn't know what happened to them."

"Surely your grandmother would have notified the authorities," Cyrus said. "She would have had someone out looking for her daughters."

"Unless they vanished. Or appeared to."

He got up and moved to the window to gaze out. "There has to be a logical explanation."

"I'm sure there is. I think you saw what really happened to my aunt in your dream—not three months ago, but thirty years ago."

Cyrus laughed as he turned back to her. "You can't believe that."

Kate pulled out the envelope she'd taken from her safe. "When I first came to town, I asked around about my mother. I knew she'd at least passed through town because of the postcard. Whitehorse was the only lead I had."

"I take it you didn't learn anything?"

"No one had heard of her and I couldn't find any evidence she was here."

"I'm sorry."

"But my efforts weren't wasted. After a few weeks of asking around, I received this." She handed him the envelope.

There was nothing written on the envelope but Cyrus could see that it had been dusted for fingerprints. He opened it and pulled out the brief note inside. The printing was childlike, almost a scrawl.

Unless you want to end up like your mother, stop looking for her.

He glanced up at Kate. "You took this to the sheriff?" he asked even though he knew she had because of the fingerprint dust.

Kate nodded. "It was a different sheriff than the one we have now. He checked it for fingerprints but said the person must have used latex gloves, which right there made me suspicious, since the only prints on the envelope or note were mine."

"But he didn't take the threat seriously," Cyrus guessed.

Kate shook her head. "He said there wasn't anything more he could do, but that I was to come to him if there were any further threats."

"And there weren't."

"No. The sheriff was convinced it was just someone fooling around, maybe even a kid."

"A kid who was smart enough to use latex gloves?"

"Exactly. That's why I think something happened to my mother here in Whitehorse to keep her from returning home. She wouldn't have just abandoned me or my grandmother."

He heard the plea in her voice. She wanted

desperately to believe that. "There hasn't been any sign of your mother since the postcard was sent from Whitehorse?"

She shook her head. "None. As I said, it's as if she simply vanished."

"If your aunt and mother simply disappeared, then how did your grandmother get your aunt's bracelet and where is your mother's?"

Kate shook her head. "My grandmother didn't have a memorial service for my aunt or mother until I was almost a year old. She told her friends that she wanted to wait until the weather was nicer. She said there was no rush since both my aunt and mother had been cremated."

"Did your grandmother say where they died?" he asked.

"Not in West Yellowstone, that's for sure," she said. "You see why I got so upset when you said it was my aunt you saw murdered here in Whitehorse."

He put the note back into the envelope. The handwriting was *childish*, but he assumed that it been on purpose. Whoever had written it had expected her to take it to the sheriff.

"You didn't do any more investigating on your own?"

Kate shook her head. "I'd hit a wall. The note made me believe I was on to something, but I didn't know what else to do. I ran my mother's photo in the newspaper. No one ever came forward."

Cyrus saw her hesitate. He watched her take a drink of her soda, then put it down on the desk before she said, "There's more. I've never told anyone, but I used to have a recurring nightmare when I was little. My mother was calling to me, trying to reach me, but something was keeping her from coming to me." She shivered as if the nightmare still gave her chills. "I could hear her voice so clearly. I never doubted it was her."

"I'm sorry. I know how real a dream can be."

She looked toward the window, hugging herself as if against the cold. "What made the nightmare so frightening for me was when my mother was calling to me I could hear something in the background…" Kate turned to look at him. "It was the sound of a baby crying. There were babies in the nursery in your dream that night, weren't there?"

"Two baby boys." He didn't mention that he saw the woman he believed was her aunt switch the babies just minutes before she was killed. "But, Kate, I dreamed it was three months ago—not thirty years. How could I have seen something while I was comatose that happened thirty years ago?"

"I don't know, but I believe you did. How else do you explain all of this?"

He couldn't explain any of it. And maybe worse, a part of him believed it.

Kate let out a sigh. "You wouldn't have come all this way and chanced looking like a fool if you didn't believe that what you saw in that dream was real."

"Right now I'm questioning my own sanity." Did he really believe dreams could reveal the future or the past? He'd come to Whitehorse because he was convinced he *hadn't* dreamed the murdered woman.

"What if it was just a bad dream, Kate, and all of this can be explained rationally?"

"You mean like explaining how it was that you recognized my aunt?" she challenged. "How old were you thirty years ago?"

"Four."

"Are you going to tell me you just happened to see her and that's how she ended up in your dream?"

"Maybe." He knew his brother, Cordell, would use that as an argument. "I was in Whitehorse thirty years ago. Maybe I saw her at the Fall Festival."

"Maybe you did. Maybe that's why the dream was so real for you, because you had seen her before."

He felt a chill snake up his spine. Was it possible that he'd remembered her all these years for some reason? *This reason,* he thought, looking at Kate.

"Cyrus, I know my mother mailed a postcard from this town thirty years ago saying she and my aunt would be coming home. My aunt was in this town. I have no idea what she was doing here or why my mother was here."

He shook his head. "I have not been able to prove one thing about my dream was true. That is why I'm so sorry that I involved you in it."

Kate smiled as she touched his arm, her gaze locking with his. "Haven't you figured it out yet? Your dream brought you here to me because together we're going to find out the truth."

He smiled back because he wanted to believe they were destined to meet. But to find a murderer? "Are you sure you want to know the truth?" he asked quietly, fearing Kate Landon didn't have any idea what she was getting into. Worse, how dangerous it might get.

"Yes, with your help," she said with a determined lift of her chin.

Cyrus appreciated her faith in him and told her as much. "The problem is that it's been thirty years. There's more than a good chance that you might never learn the truth—especially if foul play was involved. The killer has had years to cover his or her tracks."

"But there has never been a hotshot cowboy investigator looking for the truth before," she said, grinning at him.

Cyrus was flattered, but they needed hard evidence. He knew there was little chance of solving this and he'd never been the kind of man who chased rainbows—not until he'd had that damned dream.

He was reminded of the weight of the dream when he'd awakened from his coma. He'd felt such a need to tell someone. If a woman had been killed in the hospital nursery, why had he felt he had to tell anyone about it? She would have been found. It wasn't as if he'd seen the killer.

That feeling that he was meant to come here, meant to meet this woman, overwhelmed him. The answer *was* in this town, but so was the danger.

"If your aunt and mother were in Whitehorse thirty years ago, there would be some evidence of that."

"I couldn't find any," Kate said. "But from the first day I drove into town, I felt a connection to Whitehorse."

Just as he felt a connection to this woman standing before him. He could smell the sweet scent of her soap. He hoped she couldn't hear the erratic beat of his heart just at having her this near.

As she looked at him, something changed in all the emerald-green. He glimpsed a flicker of desire there, saw her slim throat work and wondered if she had been holding her breath as he had.

"It's late," he heard himself say.

She nodded. "I should go."

He nodded, knowing that if she continued to stand there looking at him like that he was going to kiss her. "We don't want the whole town talking about you and that crazy cowboy who has coma murder dreams."

"Wouldn't want that."

Cyrus walked her down to her vehicle even though she told him she would be fine. He was worried about her and not just because of his damned dream. She was putting her faith in him. He couldn't let her down. And he feared that if he kissed her, it wouldn't stop there. One day soon he had to get back to Denver and the investigations firm he ran with his brother.

He couldn't make Kate Landon any promises, and she was the kind of girl who deserved promises from a man.

"I'm glad you came to Whitehorse," she said when they reached her van.

"I hope you always feel that way," he said.

"Admit it, you believe there's a reason we both ended up here now."

He nodded, wishing the reason had only to do with the way he felt about her and not a murder—or two.

Chapter Seven

After getting very little sleep, Kate found herself going over what Cyrus had told her the night before. She had no idea how any of the pieces fit together. Babies, the hospital nursery, her mother, the postcard.

The only thing that made any sense was that Cyrus was supposed to help her find her aunt's murderer and figure out what had happened to her mother.

Kate didn't question that. She'd always believed there were things going on outside the realm of human understanding. If Cyrus had seen her aunt murdered in a dream, then Kate believed it was a message from the past.

And the fact that the dream had brought cowboy P.I. Cyrus Winchester to her meant they were to work together to solve this. She had faith that if anyone could find out the answers she so desperately needed, it was Cyrus.

At noon she put a Closed sign on the shop

door to make preparations for the haunted house that coming weekend.

But something kept nagging at her.

As she passed the glass case with her mother's bracelet in it, she had a sudden urge to take it out and look at it.

Her grandmother had told her that when her grandfather made the bracelets, he'd wanted a way that the girls could tell them apart. That was why he'd put eleven bells on one and twelve on the other. Her mother's, she recalled, had eleven on it.

With trembling fingers, she used the key to open the glass cabinet and carefully took the bracelet. It felt cool to the touch. How many times had she held this, watching the silver play in the light, and wondered about her mother?

More times than she could remember.

Kate counted the bells. Eleven. It was her mother's, then. Had her mother left it behind? Is that how her grandmother happened to have it? What other explanation could there be?

She frowned, wondering if that was what had been nagging at her, or was there something else about the bracelet? Cyrus hadn't told her why he recognized it. Had her aunt been wearing hers when he'd seen her in the dream?

Her mother and Aunt Katherine had left a hole in her life that her grandmother Dimple had done everything humanly possible to fill. And she'd always known there was more to the story than her mother's early death.

With a sigh, she put the bracelet back, closed the case and hurried downstairs. She had too much work to do on the haunted house to think about this right now.

But as she headed for the basement, Kate wondered where her aunt's bracelet was. Her grandmother, who never threw anything away, would have kept it, of course.

So why hadn't it been in the jewelry box with her mother's?

Because her grandmother had never gotten it back.

CYRUS DIDN'T HAVE any trouble finding the Ingram place north of town, although he wasn't sure why he still felt he needed to talk to Martha Ingram about that night in the old hospital.

The Ingrams lived in a newer-model home on what appeared to be a few acres.

As he got out of his pickup, he spotted an older house behind it and wondered if that was where the now deceased Wally Ingram had lived.

Martha Ingram answered his knock and welcomed him inside. She was a tall, slender woman with a head of salt-and-pepper hair and crinkles around her eyes when she smiled.

The house smelled of pumpkin bread and he was reminded again of how many months he'd lost as he let her lead him into the warm living room. Outside it was one of those cold, crisp autumn days he was familiar with in Colorado.

"You said you wanted to ask about my father?" Martha asked once they were seated and he was holding a hot cup of coffee and had tried the pumpkin bread. It was delicious.

Cyrus couldn't help feeling he was wasting this woman's time and his own. But like Kate, he couldn't understand why he'd dreamed of her aunt if there wasn't something more to it. He explained that he'd been in the hospital that night.

Martha Ingram nodded. "I remember."

"You saw me?"

"I couldn't sleep so I walked down the hall to the nurses' station. I passed your room and saw you lying there. I hope you don't mind, I asked about your condition and was told by the nurses on duty that you were in a coma from a head injury. I'm so glad that you've obviously recovered so well."

"I heard I was hooked up to a lot of equipment."

"Oh, yes. The nurses were monitoring you. My father was only on a morphine drip to make him comfortable. We knew he would be passing soon, given his declining condition. It really was a godsend."

"I'm sorry for your loss."

She shook her head. "Don't be. My father had a wonderful life. He would have said as much himself."

Cyrus liked her attitude. "Your father must have been very special."

"He was," she said, her voice breaking. "I will always miss him."

He hesitated. Why was he bothering this woman so soon after her father's death when he already knew there was no possible way he'd seen a murder that night?

Because he felt he owed it to Kate to at least try to figure this out. "Did you hear anything when you were in your father's room or on one of your walks?"

"Like what?"

"Let me be honest with you. I thought there was a murder the night I spent in the old hospital."

"A *murder?*" She looked appalled.

"Did you ever see the nurses leave their station?"

"No. There was always at least one sitting

there. As I said, they were closely monitoring you."

He saw something change in her expression. "You remembered something?"

"Well, yes, but I'm not sure if I should tell you this. I suppose it's all right. I had gone for another walk down the hall when I heard one of your monitors go off."

"Do you remember what time that was, by any chance?"

"No—wait, you know, I do. I remember looking up at the clock and being surprised at the time. It was a couple minutes after midnight. I remember thinking it felt later than that."

A couple minutes after midnight. The same time Cyrus had been convinced he'd gotten out of bed and walked down to the nursery to see the nurse's aide switch the babies—and end up murdered.

KATE WAS IN THE BASEMENT working on preparations for her haunted house when she felt a gust of cold air blow in from outside.

"Cyrus?" He'd called earlier to tell her about his plans to talk to Martha Ingram. She'd made him promise to stop by afterward to tell her how it went and had told him where she kept the spare key. "I'm down here. Cyrus?"

She listened, didn't hear anything and thought

she must have imagined someone coming in one of the doors. Still, she felt a little spooked and that surprised her. Nothing about this building had ever given her any qualms. It had been love at first sight, which just showed how rattled she was, she thought now with a smile.

The basement under the old library building was dark and dank, a warren of spooky space that she'd known the moment she saw it would make a great haunted house. There were stairways on four sides that went up to the shop level. In the center was a labyrinth of wooden structures lined with bookshelves, making the basement a maze that would allow participants to come in one way and leave by another exit.

Kate had turned on the lights but they did little to illuminate the dark corners. Over the last few weeks, Andi and Jasmine had helped her turn the basement into something that would definitely be spooky come Halloween night.

Jasmine's latest creations, a trio of ghosts, now floated on a cable above Kate's head. On Halloween they would float out of the darkness, promising to scare even the most cynical trick-or-treaters.

There were other monsters throughout the basement, including vampires, werewolves and the devil himself, who would pop up at the very end from a smoldering pit of fiery brimstone.

Andi and Jasmine had gathered volunteers to man the stations and make sure everyone got through the maze safely.

Andi had come up with little alcoves with gruesome things to touch and smell, including what appeared to be a bowl of eyeballs, a dissected brain and a boiling caldron of witch's brew straight out of *Macbeth*.

As Kate worked to make sure everything was ready and in working order, she had trouble keeping her mind on the job at hand. Her thoughts kept going to Cyrus. Last night in his hotel room there'd been that awkward moment when she'd thought he was going to kiss her.

Kissing her had probably been the last thing on his mind. She sighed. Just as Cyrus probably didn't feel what she could only describe as chemistry between them. At least on her side.

She was so involved in thought that at first she wasn't sure she heard the sound. A stair to the basement creaked.

Then she heard it again. She froze, listening. Footsteps? Hadn't she thought just moments before that she'd felt a door open? Both Andi and Jasmine had keys and Cyrus would use the spare key she'd told him about. No one else had a key and she'd made sure all the doors were locked.

With a start, she realized how asinine that

was. She hadn't had the locks replaced on the outside doors to the basement because of the expense. Who knew how many keys to this place were loose in Whitehorse from when it had been a library?

That thought did nothing for her growing anxiety. Someone was slowly coming down the basement steps.

"Hello?" she called again, still sure it had to be someone she knew just trying to scare her in her own haunted house.

She couldn't see anything from where she stood next to the soon-to-be-writhing tub of hideous-looking rubber snakes that Andi had tagged the Viper Pit.

She heard another groan, but realized it wasn't coming from the stairs. It was coming from the short landing at the top of the steps, where all the electrical boxes were kept for the building.

Kate barely had the thought when the lights went out.

CYRUS FELT HIS HEART kick up several beats at the news Martha Ingram had given him. "What did the nurses do when my monitor went off?"

"They rushed into your room," Martha Ingram said. "I heard one of them say your eyes were open and you were...very agitated. But the monitor went back to its normal beeping and the nurses came out looking relieved. I asked if you were all right and they said you were. That you'd had some kind of weird episode."

A weird episode. His heart was in his throat. "But you're sure I didn't leave my bed."

"Oh, no. I can't see how you could have in your condition and with everything that was attached to you," she said. "I stood there and talked to the nurses for probably another twenty minutes after that and you didn't move an inch. The nurses seemed worried about you and kept checking the monitors and going into your room after that to make sure you were all right." She looked chagrined. "I hope I'm not speaking out of school here. I wouldn't want to get the nurses in trouble. They were so wonderful to my father and me and so worried about you."

Cyrus nodded. "Thank you. I think this does clear things up for me."

"So was there a murder that night?" she asked with a shiver.

"No. I guess it really was nothing more than a bad dream."

Martha smiled, clearly relieved, and offered him more coffee and pumpkin bread.

"Thank you, but I should be going. I appreciate you talking with me about this."

"Well, if I've relieved your mind, then I'm glad."

On the drive back into Whitehorse, he called Cordell after finding half a dozen messages from his brother.

"Is everything all right?" Cyrus asked, afraid something had happened to his brother. Most of the investigative cases they took weren't dangerous, but you never knew when one could turn that way.

"Everything is fine here," Cordell snapped. "I've been worried sick about you. Why haven't you returned my calls?"

"I met someone."

His twin let out a laugh of relief. "So you're feeling like your old self?"

Cyrus wasn't about to tell him how he'd met Kate or what the initial attraction had been. "I'm going to stay a few more days." He listened to the silence, knowing what his brother was waiting for. "You were right. It turns out there was no murder at the hospital the night I was there, just like you and everyone else said."

"Then I'm glad you went up there to check it out," Cordell said, sounding even more relieved.

"I'm going to a haunted house on Halloween. This woman I met, Kate Landon, is putting it on."

"A haunted house? This woman sounds perfect for you."

Cyrus laughed. "We do seem to have a lot in common." Cordell didn't know the half of it, he thought as he hung up.

PITCHED INTO total blackness, Kate grabbed hold of the tub of rubber snakes, cringing as her fingers brushed one of the vipers. "This isn't funny!" she called out, her words echoing through the cavernous space. "I'm serious. Turn the lights back on. *Now.*"

On the far side of the basement she could make out a faint glow. Whoever it was had a small flashlight. She listened for a moment, feeling as if she could hear the person breathing. Her heart began to pound harder as she heard another creak of a wooden stair. Was the person leaving? Or coming down the steps toward her?

She fumbled for her cell phone, panic rising even as she told herself that no one would want to harm her. It was just a mistake. It had to be someone she knew thinking this was an amusing joke to play on her. Scare her in her own haunted house.

But at the thought of Cyrus and his murder dream, she quit kidding herself. Whoever this was— She dropped her cell phone. It fell into the huge tub of writhing snakes.

Hurriedly she felt around for it, searching frantically in all that cold rubber. No phone.

Suddenly the person stopped moving. She froze, listening to the chilling silence.

Then she heard another sound. What was that? She couldn't place it. A squeaking noise that sent fear racing up her spine.

A moment later, a loud snap filled the air, then a hissing noise.

Kate sensed something coming at her through the dark and ducked—just not soon enough. She let out a cry as she was struck so hard it knocked her to the floor. Before she could move, feeling dazed and in pain, something fell over her, covering her like a blanket. She beat at the fabric, fighting for breath, until she realized it was only the cloth ghosts that had fallen on her.

With that realization came another on its heels. The person had cut the overhead cable that held some of the props. She touched her forehead, felt a scrape where the cable had struck her.

She heard footfalls on the stairs, then the side door to the basement banged closed, then open again if the cold air that came in was any indication. In the silence that followed, she decided whoever had cut the cable was gone. She tried to get to her feet in the blinding darkness and banged into something heavy, sending stars shooting across her vision.

"KATE? KATE!"

"Down here." Something in her voice sounded all wrong to Cyrus.

"What are you doing down there in the dark?" He felt his apprehension mounting when she didn't answer. He felt around for the light switch to the basement. He'd been concerned the moment he'd seen the side door to the basement standing wide open.

This late in October, the temperature often dropped down into the teens at night and barely got up to fifty during the day. Today had been particularly chilly because of the wind. He couldn't imagine why Kate would leave the door open when she'd told him where she kept the spare key.

He'd tried to call her at the shop and hadn't been able to reach her. That had sent up red flags, since she'd said she would be working on the haunted house and had been anxious to hear how his meeting had gone with Martha Ingram. But maybe she couldn't hear the phone in the basement and hadn't taken her cell phone down with her since it went straight to voice mail.

When he'd swung by the shop he'd seen the side door standing open.

"Kate?" Cyrus called again as he found the light switch and the lights came on.

She made an angry sound, a cross between a sob and a curse.

"Kate?" He hurried down the stairs. Had she fallen? Had the power gone off? Had—

He spotted her fighting off three ghosts as she tried to get to her feet. Lying next to her along with the discarded ghosts was a thick cable coiled on the concrete floor. "What happened?"

She looked up at him and he saw where the cable had struck her forehead and realized that it must have snapped. A deep-seated fear rushed at Cyrus. He remembered the first time he'd seen her coming down the hall at the old hospital. What if his damned dream was a premonition that something was going to happen to Kate?

"Are you all right?" he asked, hurrying to her. She was trembling as he helped her to her feet and surveyed her injury. There was a bright-red scrape where the cable had hit her, bloody to the touch, but other than that, she seemed to be all right.

"Don't worry, I can fix the cable and I'll make

sure this time it doesn't come undone again," he said as he looked into her beautiful green eyes.

"It didn't come undone. Someone cut it. I heard them come in and…" She waved a hand through the air. "I pulled out my cell phone just before the person turned off the lights and cut the cable—and dropped it into the tub with the snakes."

"Here, let me," he said and felt around in the snakes until he located the phone. He handed it to her.

"I guess someone doesn't like haunted houses," she said as she turned on her phone. "I must have turned it off when I was trying to call 911."

"I guess." Cyrus felt sick. This had nothing to do with the haunted house and she damn well knew it. If he'd had any doubt that his dream meant something, he didn't anymore.

Chapter Eight

"Go ahead and say it," Kate said holding Cyrus's dark gaze. "I'm right. Or are you going to try to convince me whoever did this really doesn't like haunted houses?"

"You could have been killed," he said, sounding angry, although it was fear and concern for her behind the anger.

She'd never met anyone like this man.

"If we keep digging into this—"

"So you're just willing to drop it?" she demanded.

"Kate—"

"You know it wasn't just a dream. You've always known. You knew the moment you saw my mother's bracelet, don't deny it. You saw the bracelet in your dream, didn't you?"

He nodded slowly, reluctantly. "It was lying beside her. One of the bells had fallen off."

Kate felt her heart stop. "What?" Suddenly she felt faint again. "Are you sure?"

"What's wrong?"

"My grandfather made the bracelets a little different so my mother and aunt could tell them apart. My mother's had only eleven bells. My aunt's had twelve. The one upstairs has eleven. What if it isn't my mother's?"

He shook his head. She could tell he was as confused as she was.

"But if it's my aunt's, then how did my grandmother get it? And where is my mother's bracelet?"

"Kate, you don't want to do this," he said, lowering his voice to what felt like a caress. "I can't bear to see you hurt. Or worse."

She looked into his dark, bottomless gaze and wondered if they were still talking about the murder—or about what was happening between them. "Is that it or is it some kind of cowboy code?"

He looked confused for a moment, then realized she wasn't talking about murder. "I don't want to hurt you."

"I can take care of myself."

He dragged his Stetson from his head and raked a hand through his dark, thick hair. "Someone just tried to hurt you."

"Which proves I'm right." Kate closed the distance between them. Her palm cupped his wonderfully handsome face. She had to go up on her tiptoes to reach his mouth. Her lips brushed over his.

She could feel Cyrus's chivalrous cowboy code trying to intervene.

But she won him over as she kissed him again.

His arm looped around her waist and he dragged her to him with a groan, deepening the kiss as if, like her, he'd been wanting to do this almost since the first time he'd laid eyes on her.

A live wire of current shot through her veins, settling at her center. She felt a jolt of desire so strong it made her toes curl.

Who knows what would have happened if her cell phone hadn't rung.

Cyrus drew back, looking shaken by the kiss and the desire he couldn't hide in his gaze. "You'd better answer that," he said, sounding breathless.

She glanced at the caller ID. It was Andi and it was marked urgent.

CYRUS WATCHED KATE take the call, both relieved and sorry for the interruption. He knew instinctively that Kate wasn't the kind of woman who took making love with a man lightly. And because of that he couldn't possibly let it happen.

After Halloween he had to get back to Denver, get back to work, get back to his life.

But the thought came with a strange feeling of regret. After coming out of the coma, he'd been anxious to get to Montana and find out the truth about his murder dream. But then he'd always known he would go back to Winchester Investigations. He enjoyed his work and normally would be champing at the bit to get back to it.

However, nothing had been normal since he'd seen Kate in the old hospital hallway. He had a feeling nothing would be normal again.

Still, as she hung up the phone, he reminded himself of all the reasons kissing Kate again would be a very bad idea. Because he knew that what he wanted more than anything was to make love to this woman and one more kiss…

As she stuck the cell phone into her jacket pocket, she said, "That was my friend Andi. She's a reporter for the *Milk River Examiner*, our local weekly newspaper, and she just found what she believes is the only murder ever committed at the old hospital."

"Kate—" Cyrus wasn't even sure what he'd planned to say. No doubt an apology for kissing her the way he had. But she didn't give him a chance.

"Don't you see what this means?" she demanded, waving an arm to encompass the basement. For a moment he thought she was talking about the kiss, about the passion that had sparked between them. "Whoever cut that cable doesn't want us finding out what really happened to my aunt and my mother. This proves it and now Andi has found an old murder she said she thinks we'll be interested in."

He couldn't believe this. She was just going to ignore the kiss, ignore what had just happened between them? He knew damn well she'd felt it, too. Or, like him, was she afraid to look too closely at whatever was developing between them? If anything?

Kate was looking at him as if she couldn't understand why he was still standing there, why he wasn't excited about this news. She obviously was.

He stared at her. "This doesn't prove anything," he said, finding himself wanting to grab her and kiss some sense into her. "Except that, because of me, someone wants to hurt you."

"They must think I know something."

"But you don't know anything and neither do I. Except that there wasn't a murder the night I spent in the old hospital."

Her green gaze locked with his. She grinned at him, completely disarming him. "Don't look so upset," Kate said, brushing a lock of his hair back from his forehead. The tips of her fingers grazed his skin, shattering his senses. "This is good news. It proves you aren't crazy. Take some encouragement in that."

He shook his head, unable to resist her. "I have never met anyone like you, Kate Landon."

"Trust me, you're my first psychic cowboy."

"If I were psychic I'd have seen that someone was going to cut the cable that hit you." *And I'd know what was going to happen with the two of us,* he thought, wishing for the first time that he was psychic. Then he would know if Kate was going to be safe.

"Let me say this again," he said. "Someone just tried to hurt you, possibly even kill you. If it really was about your aunt's death and your mother's disappearance, then us digging around in it could get you killed. I can't let that happen."

She smiled. "But you also can't stop me."

"Kate—"

"I need to get over to the newspaper. Are you coming or not?"

He looked into her eyes and knew that he would follow her anywhere, anytime. They were in this together. At least until he found out who had tried to hurt her. He had a bad feeling he already knew why.

ANDI LIFTED A BROW and mouthed "Hottie!" when Kate came into the newspaper office with

Cyrus Winchester. Andi's expression changed, though, the moment she saw where the cable had connected with Kate's forehead. "What happened to you?"

"A little accident in the basement while she was finishing up the haunted house," Cyrus said. "I don't believe we've met." He held out his hand. "Kate has told me all about you."

Andi arched a brow as she shook his hand. "I've heard a lot about you, as well."

"I'll bet you have," Cyrus said and laughed. It was deep and throaty and Kate loved the sound. She looked over at him as he shoved back his Stetson. The man really was gorgeous. And boy, could he kiss. Her toes curled at the memory of being in his arms.

"I thought you might be interested in the only documented murder I could find at the old hospital," Andi said and led them back to the archives at the back of the small newspaper office.

Since the paper had gone out the day before, the office was nearly deserted except for a young woman doing billing.

The headline on the newspaper article Andi had found jumped out at Kate, making her heart begin to pound.

Nurse Found Murdered in Hospital

Her gaze flew to the date. Dec. 19, 1980.

Thirty years ago. She gripped the back of the chair in front of the microfiche. Then her gaze focused on the victim's name: Candace Porter.

She frowned. The name meant nothing to her.

As Andi moved the microfiche so they could see the rest of the story, a photograph of a dark-haired woman came up.

Kate almost didn't recognize her aunt. Katherine looked so different from the photographs she'd seen of her when she'd had blond hair. But there was no doubt. Candace Porter and Katherine Landon were the same woman.

The same murdered woman—straight from Cyrus Winchester's dream, only thirty years ago, just as she'd feared.

Suddenly her legs seemed to give out. She felt Cyrus's large, warm hands grab her and ease her down into a spare chair behind Andi. He'd seen the photograph of the murdered nurse. He'd recognized her aunt.

"It doesn't say how the woman was killed," Andi was saying, unaware of the drama going on behind her. "In fact there is little information. There's a follow-up story, but apparently the woman wasn't from around here. There's no apparent next of kin. No wonder I'd never heard of this."

Her aunt had been murdered at the hospital

one night—just like in Cyrus's dream. But she hadn't been going by her real name. Was it possible her grandmother hadn't known the truth of what had happened to Katherine and that was why she'd made up the story about the weak heart?

"What about the killer?" Cyrus asked Andi.

"Apparently never caught," Andi said. "The only other story I found about the murder was a follow-up twenty years ago on the tenth anniversary of the woman's death. The murderer was still at large."

"Can you make me a copy of the stories?" Cyrus asked.

"Sure," Andi said. "So is this exactly like your dream?" Cyrus didn't answer and Andi looked back at Kate. "Are you all right?"

Kate could only nod. She knew eventually she would tell Andi everything, but not now. Not when she was too upset to discuss it.

"Kate's still a little dazed from being hit by the cable," Cyrus said.

Kate could tell that Andi was bursting at the seams to ask more questions.

"I should get you home," Cyrus said to Kate. "She took a pretty good hit on the head," he told Andi.

Andi nodded. "I can't believe that cable would break. Maybe we should use something else."

"Don't worry," Cyrus said. "I'll fix it so there is no chance it will fall on anyone again."

"So do you think this is the murder you thought you saw?" Andi asked Cyrus again as she walked them to the door.

He shrugged. "I think it's a coincidence, but kind of interesting," he said, playing it down.

"That would be wild if you dreamed a murder that took place thirty years ago," Andi said. "If that turns out to be the case—"

"You'll be the first to get the story," Cyrus said as he folded the copies of the articles and put them in his jacket pocket.

Kate felt Andi's gaze on her. "Maybe you should swing by the hospital and have a doctor check you out."

It wasn't until she and Cyrus were outside in the brisk fall air that she felt she could breathe. "I don't understand."

"Me neither, but then I've been confused about this since the beginning. Let's talk about it back at the shop."

She shivered as she saw him glance around as if he thought someone might be watching them. He put his arm around her and they started back toward Second Hand Kate's.

The main drag had been decorated with cornstalks and pumpkins and, while there were Halloween decorations in most of the windows,

Christmas music played from a few of the stores they passed.

Kate found herself watching the people who drove past them in a way she'd never noticed anyone before. She tried not to think about what this all meant. Her head ached but she still noticed that Cyrus seemed even more worried about her than he had earlier.

Her aunt had been *murdered.*

Why had that come as a shock to either of them? Cyrus had seen her aunt dead in the hospital nursery. And all her life Kate had felt there was more to the story. Still, seeing it in print...

"Is there any reason the front door of your shop would be open?" Cyrus asked, jerking her from her thoughts.

Kate turned to look. The door was ajar. "My friend Jasmine might—"

"Stay here," Cyrus ordered as he pulled a gun from a shoulder holster under his jacket and ran toward her open shop door. Had he been wearing the gun since he'd come to town? Or had he only put it on after the cable incident? He'd gone to his pickup while she'd changed clothes...

Kate had never been good at doing what she was told. She was right behind him when he eased the front door all the way open, and she saw the broken glass sparkling on the rich patina of the old wooden floor—and Jasmine.

CYRUS RACED toward the dark-haired young woman standing in the middle of the room with a fireplace poker gripped in both hands. The woman lowered the poker the moment she saw Kate behind him and burst into tears.

"I scared him away," the woman said through her sobs.

"Oh, Jasmine," Kate said, pushing past him to hug her friend.

"Him?" Cyrus asked after Jasmine calmed down a little. He'd surveyed the damage and found that the only thing that looked as if it had been broken into was the glass case that held Kate's mementos.

The silver bracelet was still where it had been. Apparently Jasmine had scared the robber away before he could get what he'd come for. Assuming, of course, he'd been after the bracelet.

It made little sense to steal the bracelet. There wouldn't be any evidence on it after thirty years. That was also assuming there was something to his dream and Candace Porter, aka Katherine Landon, had actually been wearing the bracelet when she died.

So far, the only details he could verify from his "dream" were that the woman he'd seen actually had died in the old hospital nursery—but it just happened to be thirty years ago on December 19, 1980.

That and, as Kate had pointed out, asking about the old murder had someone in town apparently stirred up enough to attack her—and break into her shop.

"You said 'him.' You're sure it was definitely a man you saw?" Cyrus asked Jasmine again.

By now they were all sitting around Kate's red-checked 1950s table upstairs, Jasmine cupping a mug of hot chocolate. While red-eyed, she seemed to have pulled herself together.

Kate had insisted they come upstairs while they waited for the sheriff to arrive so she could make hot chocolate as she said her grandmother always did when she was sad or upset.

She handed Cyrus a cup and took a seat across from him at the table she said she'd found at a farm auction north of town. There was something so cozy and serene about the upstairs apartment—in vivid contrast to the tension in the room.

He watched Kate close her eyes and take a sip of the hot chocolate, a large melting marshmallow floating on top. It reminded him of last night at the frybread stand.

She'd made the top floor into a three-bedroom apartment. There was plenty of room in the high-ceilinged space and it was clear she'd let herself go, decorating it with some of her favorite finds.

He had removed his Stetson and held the large mug of hot chocolate with both hands now. Like Jasmine, he felt he needed the warmth.

"Why don't you start at the beginning," Kate suggested to Jasmine as she shot Cyrus a look to be patient.

Jasmine took a shuddering breath and let it out slowly. "I let myself in with the key you gave me. I didn't turn on a light because I didn't want anyone to think the shop was open. As I headed for the basement…" She took a sip of the hot chocolate. "This is really good," she said to Kate, who beamed and said, "Thank you."

"So you came in and headed for the basement," Cyrus nudged gently. "In the dark?"

Jasmine blinked. "It wasn't dark. I remember now. There was a light on upstairs."

He glanced over at Kate. She shook her head that she hadn't left a light on.

"Then what happened?"

"I glanced upstairs, but didn't hear anything, so I assumed you had just left a light on for when you came home. Then I opened the basement door and started to go down the steps." She paused to put down her mug. "I was about halfway down when I heard someone upstairs.

I thought it was you." She smiled over at Kate. "So I went back downstairs feeling weird, you know. That's when I heard the sound of breaking glass."

"The intruder must not have heard you come in," Kate said and reached across the table to cover her friend's hand with her own. "I'm so sorry you had to go through this."

"So then what did you do?" Cyrus asked.

"I called to Kate from the basement stairs where I had stopped again, asking if she was all right. I just assumed she'd come home and dropped something." Jasmine shrugged apologetically. "When she didn't answer and it got real quiet, I had a bad feeling. I came upstairs. I was just passing the room with the wonderful old fireplace...did Kate tell you that I helped her strip off all the old paint on the mantel?"

"We hadn't gotten to that yet," Cyrus said, feeling Kate's imploring gaze on him, asking him again to be patient with her friend. "That's where you found the poker, right?"

Jasmine nodded. "I grabbed it and came out to the main room to find the front door open and glass all over the floor."

"You scared him away before he could do any more damage, apparently," Cyrus said. "You said *him,* but you never saw the person?"

Jasmine shook her head. "I just assumed it

was a man. A woman would not break the glass on that beautiful case."

Cyrus smiled to himself, thinking of the investigations he'd been involved in where a woman had done much more than break a little glass.

Kate got up to get her friend more hot chocolate.

"I'd like you to look around and make sure nothing else was taken before the sheriff gets here," Cyrus said to Kate.

He could tell she was shaken by the break-in and her friend's near run-in with a burglar. But he suspected it was nothing after what they'd seen at the newspaper—the picture of a murder victim who Kate had been told had died from a weak heart.

AT CYRUS'S INSISTENCE, Kate went through the shop and her apartment upstairs, looking for anything out of place or missing. She was more upset than she'd let on. Angry and scared. Not just angry and upset. She hadn't wanted to fall apart when Jasmine needed her to hold it together. Nor did she want Cyrus to see how upset she really was after what she'd seen in the newspaper.

When she'd seen her friend standing there with a poker in her hands... Kate was just thankful that Jasmine hadn't confronted the burglar.

She felt violated just knowing that someone had gone through her things and at the same time thankful for her friend and Cyrus. He was downstairs now, inspecting the locks and windows to see if he could find out how the intruder had gotten in.

"With all the wonderful things you have sitting around, I'm surprised he didn't take anything," Jasmine said, frowning at her from across the room. They'd gone through the shop and found nothing missing. Not even from the broken case.

Now, back upstairs, Kate spotted the first thing she'd found out of place in her apartment, even though it was clear whoever had broken in had been looking for something.

"What is it?" Jasmine asked, seeing her reaction.

"My photos," Kate said in a voice that broke. She rushed to it but stopped herself from snatching up the album. "Fingerprints. There could be fingerprints," she said to herself out loud.

Going in the kitchen she pulled a wooden spoon from the canister by the stove and returned to the album the burglar had left out.

Using the handle of the spoon, she carefully opened it. Her heart thudded in her chest. Hadn't she known what would be missing the moment she saw that the intruder had pulled down the photos?

"What's going on?" Cyrus asked as he came into the room.

"I think the burglar took some of Kate's photographs," Jasmine said. "Why would he break in to take photos and try to steal something out of your memento case? That doesn't make a whole lot of sense."

It did to Kate. She looked at Cyrus as she let the album fall open on the page with the missing photographs of her aunt and mother and saw that it made sense to him, as well.

Chapter Nine

Sheriff McCall Winchester had known it was just a matter of time before she met her cousin Cyrus. She'd heard he was in town asking a lot of crazy questions. Some of the same questions she'd already answered for his brother when he'd called from Denver asking about a murder.

Rumors were flying and Cyrus Winchester was now the talk of the town.

Given all that, she hadn't been that surprised to get a call from him about a break-in at Second Hand Kate's. Since meeting his twin, Cordell, she'd come to expect wherever the Winchester men went, trouble was never far behind.

"It's nice to finally meet you," McCall said as she shook Cyrus's hand upon arriving at the shop. One of her deputies was busy shooting the scene and checking for prints. "I visited you a few times in the hospital, but I'm sure you don't remember."

"No, sorry." He had the Winchester dark eyes

and hair just like her. She saw him studying her, no doubt seeing the Winchester resemblance, and had to smile. Fortunately she looked like their grandmother, but it had taken Pepper's acceptance to make people quit questioning her birthright. "You're Uncle Trace's daughter?"

She smiled. "Not all the stories about my mother turned out to be true."

He seemed to relax. "I was sorry to hear about your father."

McCall nodded. Finding out that her father hadn't abandoned her mother and her before she was born had been a double-edged sword. Trace Winchester hadn't run off—he had gotten himself murdered. Either way, she'd never known her father.

"Why don't I start with Jasmine and Kate, if you don't mind hanging around until I'm finished with them," McCall said.

"I'll be right here."

She smiled, sensing that protectiveness she'd seen in his brother and wondering how it was that he and Kate had met. All in good time, she thought as she went upstairs to where the other two were waiting.

"Why don't you step in here, Cyrus," McCall suggested a while later. She motioned to one of the small rooms in the shop that had been decorated as a parlor, much like the real one at her grandmother's lodge on the Winchester Ranch.

"I've heard Jasmine's and Kate's stories as to the break-in," McCall continued. "I can't wait to hear yours, since Kate tells me it has to do with her aunt and mother and some dream you had while in the coma."

"We don't know that for a fact," he hedged, but at her prodding recounted his dream.

She listened as he told her about what he'd thought he'd seen at the hospital and how the woman had been wearing the silver bracelet he'd seen in the glass cabinet—the same cabinet someone had broken into but either hadn't been after the bracelet or had gotten scared away before taking it. A bracelet that could have belonged to Kate's aunt rather than her mother.

McCall raised a brow when he told her about the newspaper article. The woman named Candace Porter had been murdered just like in his dream—and she had turned out to be Kate's aunt, Katherine Landon, only she was going by an assumed name.

"Kate and I both recognized her," Cyrus said.

"And it was her photo and Kate's mother's photographs that were taken from the album upstairs." McCall got the feeling he was leaving something out and wondered why. Perhaps to protect Kate? There was definitely something going on between Cyrus and Kate.

"How exactly did you meet Kate?" she asked and could have sworn he blushed. She listened as he told her about seeing her at the hospital and thinking she was the woman from his dream, only to realize she had to be a relative of the dead woman.

McCall couldn't miss the way he talked about Kate. *These Winchester men,* she thought with no small amount of amusement, since her father had broken more than a few hearts, including her mother's.

"Wow, that was some dream," she said when Cyrus finished. "So you've been asking a bunch of questions around town about a murder and now you think the murderer broke in here, took some photographs and tried to take the bracelet."

"Believe me, I wish it had been nothing more than a bad dream. There was a point where I was starting to believe it was—even against all odds."

"Until you found Kate in the basement after someone cut the cable and Andi found the newspaper article about a thirty-year-old murder at the hospital, and now this break-in." McCall studied him. "Nothing else was taken besides some family photographs?"

He shook his head. "Apparently not."

"This silver bell bracelet that you saw in your dream, is it the same one in the case that was broken?"

"It looks pretty similar. Apparently there were two bracelets. Kate's grandfather made them for his daughters. Whoever broke in must have seen the bracelet, recognized it and thought..." He hesitated. "Who knows what he—or she—thought."

"Or *she?*"

"Jasmine didn't see the person. I wouldn't rule out that it might have been a woman. Whoever cut the cable wasn't particularly strong. When I inspected the cable just before you arrived, I noticed that it had taken several attempts to cut it."

"Interesting." McCall had heard Cyrus and Cordell were damned good private investigators in Denver. She'd gotten the chance to work with his brother in June and could attest to how devoted they were. Both had almost gotten killed. "So what's your theory?"

"I just got over thinking I was crazy. I was hoping you'd look into the Candace Porter murder. She was apparently killed in the nursery at the old hospital. She was a nurse, according to the story, but Kate says she's sure her aunt never went to nursing school. Unfortunately, we don't have any photographs of her—other than the one in the newspaper article. Whoever broke in took them."

"But you and Kate are sure Candace Porter was her aunt, Katherine Landon?"

"Yes. The same woman I dreamed about while in my coma. Don't ask me to explain it."

"Very strange," McCall agreed, thinking this could be the strangest investigation she'd come across yet. "I'll see what I can find out."

As Cyrus walked McCall to the door, she asked the one question he'd been dreading. "Have you been out to see Grandmother?" He must have raised a brow, because she laughed.

"Yeah, it still seems odd calling her *Grandmother,* but she's accepted that I'm one of you," McCall said. "Not sure that's a good thing, but she seems to be trying to make up for the past."

"You think that's why she invited my brother and me back here?"

"No," she said with a laugh. "From what I can gather it has something to do with my father's murder. I don't believe she's happy with the outcome of the investigation. Which is probably how I became acting sheriff—until the election, at least. Not that she isn't above interfering with the election to get what she wants."

He had to smile at her honesty. "Doesn't sound like Pepper can put much over on you."

"Our grandmother gets whatever she wants one way or another, but I probably don't have to tell you that."

"No," he admitted. "I heard from Cordell that she seems to think someone in the family was involved in your father's death." He saw from McCall's expression that there might be something to that and felt sick inside at the thought. He knew his father, Brand, wasn't involved, but wouldn't put anything past his Aunt Virginia.

"These things have a way of coming out in time," McCall said.

"Didn't I hear you're getting married in December at Winchester Ranch?"

She laughed. "That's probably when Grandmother will drop her bombshell, huh? I've thought of that. But doesn't every bride want a wedding she will never forget? You should go see her. Maybe I'm wrong, but I think she isn't as uncaring as she pretends to be."

"I might before I leave."

"So you'll be staying around for a while?"

"For a while," he said noncommittally. He couldn't leave now because of Kate and whatever was going on, even if he wanted to.

At the back of his mind a part of him still worried that the dream wasn't about getting justice in a thirty-year-old murder case. It was a premonition that Kate was the real victim he'd come to Whitehorse to save—or die trying.

"YOU TOLD THE SHERIFF about your dream?" Kate asked Cyrus, still feeling shaken. She'd cleaned up the broken glass after Jasmine, the sheriff and her deputy had left.

Cyrus had gone around the house making sure the place was locked up for the night. He'd composed a list of locks that needed to be changed and security measures to be added.

"She's going to see what she can find out about Candace Porter. I'm sorry, Kate."

She nodded. Growing up, she'd believed she could handle most anything. She'd already lost her mother and aunt all those years ago, and recently her grandmother.

But it had been one thing to believe there was merit to Cyrus's dream and another to find out that her aunt had really been murdered, then right on the heels of that to find her shop broken into, her treasured photographs taken and the bracelet nearly gone, as well.

Not to mention that whoever was involved might still be in Whitehorse after thirty years—

and knew not only who she was, but that she and Cyrus were looking into her aunt's murder.

"They were looking for something, weren't they?"

"That's my thought, but what? Whoever it was recognized the bracelet. I think that is why they decided to take it as they were leaving. I remember my reaction when I noticed it on my way out the first time. The killer must have been shocked to see it, as well."

"Which means my aunt's killer is still in town," Kate said.

"It would seem so."

"What could the person have been looking for?"

"I would imagine the killer thinks we must have some kind of evidence. Otherwise, how could I know the things I do?"

"Your dream," she said with a nod. "The killer thinks you made that part up."

"I wish."

"Maybe there is evidence," she said suddenly. "I need to go to West Yellowstone to my grandmother's cabin. After she died I couldn't go through all her things. I started, but the woman was a pack rat. I doubt she ever threw anything away. It was just too overwhelming. But now, I can't help but wonder what else she kept from me."

"Well, I'm going with you. I'm not letting you out of my sight until this is over."

She liked the sound of that. Except for the "until this is over" part.

"I probably should mention that West Yellowstone is seven hours from here. If we leave now we'll get there late but we can stay over, if you don't mind."

"Sure." Cyrus looked worried and she wondered if, like her, he was thinking about the two of them alone in a cabin in the woods and that kiss.

Or maybe that was the last thing on his mind.

"Thank you for going with me," she said. In truth, she wasn't sure she could have faced this alone.

As she quickly packed to leave, she couldn't get out of her head that her aunt had lived and worked in Whitehorse. No wonder her mother had sent the postcard from here. But why would her aunt have been using another name? And how was it that her aunt was working as a nurse? Kate was almost certain Katherine had never been to nursing school.

Kate suddenly remembered one of Dimple's friends telling her about her aunt once at a wedding, after her grandmother's friend had had too much champagne. "Katherine was your grandmother's wild child," the friend said in confidence. "Your mother made up for it. Elizabeth was the perfect child. Do you know what she did? When she was little she would take the blame for things her sister did, just to protect Katherine."

Is that why her mother had left her so soon after she was born to come to Whitehorse? Had Katherine been in trouble? Kate could only assume so, given that Katherine hadn't been using her real name.

What else would Kate discover about her aunt and her mother once they got to West Yellowstone?

Whatever trouble her aunt had gotten into thirty years ago, it apparently was still in town, Kate thought as she glanced toward her broken glass case. She'd taken her mementos out for safekeeping. The bracelet was now in her purse.

The photographs of her aunt and mother were gone and it broke her heart. But she thought the person responsible had left them a clue.

"The burglar took both my mother's and my aunt's photographs," she said to Cyrus. "Why would he take both?"

"Maybe he couldn't tell them apart."

"Or maybe he knew my mother." She just hoped the answer was somewhere in her grand-mother's cabin.

MCCALL COULDN'T BELIEVE all the things she was supposed to do just to get married, and said as much to her fiancé, Luke, later that afternoon.

"We could elope," he suggested.

She looked at him to see if he was serious, because at that moment she would have taken him up on it.

He quickly shook his head as if he knew her too well. "It's going to be a beautiful wedding that we will remember the rest of our lives."

She laughed. "That's what I'm afraid of."

He pulled her into his arms. "You deserve this wedding."

"Still scaring me. I know you're worried about what my grandmother might be up to as much as I am."

"Honey," he said after kissing her. "We're getting married at the Winchester Ranch. It's what your father would have wanted, and if you don't go through with it, your mother will never forgive you."

That convinced her. Ruby *would* never forgive her. "You're right."

"Not to mention your grandmother seems

more excited about your wedding than anyone—even us. I really think she wants to welcome you to the family."

"I went to pick out flowers. Luke, there are too many decisions to make without some help."

He looked panicked, as if he was worried she would ask him to go along. "How about your mother?"

"Ruby?" McCall cried. "She'd want plastic flowers, large, bright ones."

"You need to give your mother more credit."

"You think? The other day she suggested that she thought it would be cool if she and I had a double wedding at the ranch."

"Are she and Red to that point?"

McCall shrugged. Her mother had been dating Red for a few months, longer than most of her boyfriends lasted. "Can you imagine what my grandmother would have to say about Ruby getting married at the ranch? It's going to be nerve-racking enough just having Ruby and Pepper in the same room for our wedding."

"They both want you to be happy. Neither would dream of spoiling the wedding."

She wished she shared his optimism.

"I heard there was a break-in at Second Hand Kate's."

She told him about it and about her cousin

Cyrus's dream—and the murdered nurse going by the name of Candace Porter.

"Are you telling me he saw a murder that happened thirty years ago while he was in a coma?" Luke asked, looking as skeptical as she'd first felt.

"A woman was murdered who, according to her niece, looks exactly like her aunt," McCall said. "But that isn't the worst part of all this. I suspect there is something Cyrus is holding back. I think it might be the killer's motive."

CYRUS WATCHED the landscape change from the rolling prairie where thousands of buffalo once roamed to mountain ranges, dark green with pines. The wind howled across the open spaces, bending over the tall yellowed grasses as antelope dotted the hillsides and eagles soared on the thermals.

The two-lane highway dropped southward, the majestic Beartooth mountain range coming up out of the horizon like a mirage. They turned at the Crazy Mountains, caught Interstate 90 and headed west toward Bozeman as the sun sank. As other mountain ranges came into view, all were dusted with snow, another sign that winter wasn't far off.

They stopped in Bozeman for lunch and were just heading for the Gallatin Canyon, which would take them to West Yellowstone, when his cell phone rang.

"Cyrus?" He recognized the sheriff's voice and glanced over at Kate. McCall had found out something or she wouldn't be calling. "Where are you?"

"On our way to Kate's grandmother's cabin in West Yellowstone. She thinks the answers might be there."

"I tracked down Candace Porter, the *real* Candace Porter," the sheriff said. "She used to be a nurse at a hospital in Missoula, Montana. Her purse was stolen the day of her going-away party. She was headed for Paris, where her fiancé was living. The two of them were planning to travel around Europe before settling down."

"Let me guess. Katherine Landon worked at the same hospital."

"Bingo. She was a nurse's aide before she miraculously became a nurse by the name of Candace Porter."

Cyrus had suspected it might be something like this. "Was Candace Porter's family ever contacted after the murder?"

"No next of kin could be found. She was buried here in Whitehorse."

"Thanks for letting me know. We'll be back tomorrow, probably late."

"Don't worry. We're keeping an eye on the shop, but if you're right about what the burglar was after, then I doubt there will be another break-in."

He agreed. For a moment he thought about telling McCall what else he'd seen that night in his dream—Katherine Landon switching the two baby boys in bassinets in the hospital nursery, but he didn't want to do it on the phone. "Thanks" was all he said before he hung up.

Cyrus realized it felt like a betrayal to say anything to the sheriff about the babies until they had some evidence that the babies had even existed. He realized the ramifications if the babies had been switched as they had been in his dream. Both of the boys would be thirty now. What a time to find out that the parents you'd known all your life weren't really your parents. He'd heard of a case or two like that. He couldn't imagine how it would affect not only the parents, but also the young men.

He couldn't, however, keep what McCall had told him from Kate, even though he knew she wasn't going to like hearing it.

"I suspected as much given that she wasn't using her real name," Kate said after he told her. He could see she was taking the news much worse than she let on. "I wonder if my mother knew about her sister stealing another person's identity, pretending to be a nurse?"

"I suspect it might be why she left you to go to Whitehorse. Clearly your aunt was in over her head. Kate, there is something I haven't told you that I saw in my dream. I saw her switch the babies in the bassinets."

Kate stared at him in disbelief. "Why would she do that?" He shook his head. "Did you tell the sheriff?"

"I'll have to if we find any evidence that it really happened."

Kate was silent for a few minutes, as if taking it in. "You think that's what got her killed. Someone put her up to the baby switch. But why would they turn around and kill her?"

Because they didn't want a witness who could come forward years later, he was about to suggest.

"But what if she was switching the babies back, what if she'd changed her mind?" Kate said. She had a point.

"I suppose, depending on the deal that was made, that could have gotten her killed," he said.

"Maybe my mother talked her out of it."

He could see that's what she wanted to believe.

"And it got them both killed."

Cyrus thought she could be right. He just hoped they would find what they needed in West Yellowstone.

THE DRIVE DOWN the narrow Gallatin Canyon through the mountains in October was beautiful. The highway followed the Gallatin River, with its crystal-clear water rushing over large granite rocks. The trees had turned to an array of golds, reds and rusts, and now the breeze showered the cold river with the colorful leaves. Caught in the current, they floated quickly downstream.

During the drive, Kate talked about what it had been like growing up in West Yellowstone with her grandmother. "I loved living in a tourist town when I was a kid. Summers were wild and crazy with the town packed with people. They used to have street dances in front of the old Texaco gas station and one of the bars used to pipe the music from the bands out onto the street."

Beside the highway, a few fly-fishermen braved the chilly day to cast long, sleek lines out over the deep, cold green of the river.

"I would imagine winters were quite different there," he said as they passed Big Sky, the snow-capped Lone Peak spectacular against the clear blue sky.

"It wasn't like now, but snowmobiles definitely

changed things," she said. "It was how we got around town. There were trails on top of the huge drifts where the snow had been plowed." Kate smiled in memory. "We used to run all over at night in the cold, snowy darkness. It really was a wonderland."

"I'm surprised you didn't go back after college," Cyrus said.

"The town changed for me. Or maybe I was the one who changed. I guess that's why I love Whitehorse. I like the small-town feel."

"Whitehorse suits you."

She laughed. "Thanks. I agree." Then she sobered. "No matter what we find out, I won't be leaving Whitehorse."

Yes, he thought, he'd known that when he'd seen her shop. She'd found herself a home. He knew she would hate Denver.

The canyon opened at the top of Fir Ridge for a view of Hebgen Lake, the surface golden, in the distance. Then the road ran through the dense pines into town.

West, as the locals called it, was a small tourist town on the edge of Yellowstone Park. It sat among tall pines, a mix of old log cabins and new motels and businesses. Once a town that boarded up and closed all but a few businesses in winter, it was now a mecca for snowmobilers who wanted to see Yellowstone in its frosty-white season. This time of the year, though, things were pretty quiet as everyone waited for snow.

KATE'S GRANDMOTHER'S CABIN sat back in the tall pines, rustic and rambling, on one of the lots at the edge of town. Past the property the trees and land ran east to hit the boundary of Yellowstone Park.

"My grandmother left the place to me," Kate said as she opened the door. "I don't get down here much, but I can't part with it. I grew up here. It's a part of me."

"I envy you," Cyrus said. "This cabin is wonderful. There is no place that I could really call home—not since my grandmother kicked us all off the ranch."

"I'm sorry," she said, studying him for a moment. "Everyone needs a place to call home."

"We moved a lot when I was growing up," he said as he brought in their bags and set them down in the living room. "My father worked on different ranches across the west. So I got used to things being temporary."

"Not even Denver feels like home?"

He chuckled. "Maybe especially Denver."

Kate looked around the cabin. Now that she was here, she didn't know what to do.

"You said your grandmother saved everything," Cyrus commented. "You weren't kidding."

"Because of that I have no idea where to start." She couldn't help sounding discouraged. It had been a long drive. She was tired. But probably more than anything she was afraid of what they were going to find here.

"We don't have to do this tonight," he said. "We could wait until the morning if you want."

She shook her head. "There is so much to go through—it is still early enough."

"Okay. How about those files?" he said, pointing to three metal file cabinets next to a desk in what appeared to be a small office.

She put down her purse but didn't move.

"You sure you want to do this?" he asked as she only stared at the filing cabinets.

"Yes." She gave herself a push and stepped to the first cabinet and pulled open the top drawer. "Oh, this is not going to be easy."

"You take one drawer and I'll take one," he suggested. "Anything from thirty years ago."

She nodded as he carried the top drawer to the kitchen table. Kate sat next to the drawer he'd put there for her and pulled out the first manila file folder.

Cyrus went for the next drawer, bringing it

back to sit down across from her. It was like searching for a needle in a haystack, but she didn't know what else to do.

It was a little after 10:00 p.m. when Kate found the letters. She froze, her fingers trembling as she read the name the letter was addressed to: Elizabeth Landon. The postmark was Whitehorse, Montana, dated Dec. 12, 1980.

"Cyrus." That was all she could get out.

He came to her at once. She handed him the envelope, he glanced at it, then started to hand it back.

She shook her head. "Would you read it, please?"

He nodded, pulled the letter from the envelope, unfolded it and quickly read through it before he handed it to her.

Kate didn't look at it, just at him. "Tell me."

"Your aunt said she needed her sister. Just for a little while. She wanted her to come to Whitehorse. She'd done something and she feared this time she was in real trouble. She said she'd exaggerated on her employment application and her boss had found out. But it was more complicated than that."

Even though Kate had known this must have been what happened, she still had trouble believing it. "Didn't my aunt realize that I was just a baby? She'd gotten herself into this mess and she drags my mother into it?"

Kate shoved back from the table and stormed into the living room, only to stop because there was no place to run from this. Angry tears burned her eyes.

"I can't believe my mother would go," she said, fighting to keep from crying. She heard Cyrus rise from the table and come up behind her.

"I can," he said softly. "If my brother was in trouble, I'd be there tomorrow. He'd do the same for me."

"But to bail out a sister like Katherine? I'd heard she was always in trouble. Lying about being a nurse..." Kate shook her head. "Couldn't she have gone to jail over that?"

"Possibly," he said, putting his large, warm hands on her shoulders and turning her around to face him. "Sometimes with siblings it's a love-hate relationship, but when push comes to shove, especially if that sibling is in some serious trouble, then you're going to be there. Your mother had to make a difficult choice, but she knew you would be fine with your grandmother."

Kate nodded and made a swipe at her tears. "I envy that kind of relationship."

"Your grandmother was like that with you. She hid the truth from you to protect you."

"I know."

He bent down a little to look into her face. "We can stop this right now."

"No," Kate said. "We can't. My aunt said in that letter that her boss had found out about her not being a nurse, and yet she was still working at the hospital?"

CYRUS HAD THOUGHT the same thing. If Katherine had been caught then she should have been fired immediately. Why hadn't she been?

He couldn't wait to get back to Whitehorse and ask the hospital administrator, Roberta Warren.

Kate took the letter from him. He watched her read through it. He could tell she was exhausted. "It's late," he said.

She nodded. "I think I will call it a night. Take any bedroom you want. I made up the beds with clean sheets the last time I was here." She glanced toward the table. "There are more letters…"

"I can take a look at them and see if there is anything in them," he offered.

Her emerald gaze filmed over with tears again. "Thank you."

Kate looked into his handsome face and lost a little piece of her heart to Cyrus Winchester. He was so kind and caring and she didn't know what she would have done without him being here with her.

She thought about the first time she'd seen him standing in the old hospital hallway. Cyrus Winchester in his jeans and boots, western shirt and Stetson. She hadn't been able to get that image out of her mind, or shake the feeling then that he was in some kind of trouble.

Is this the way her mother had felt about her sister? Is this why she had to leave Kate to go to Katherine?

"Cyrus…" Words failed her as she was filled with love for this man and understood how feeling like this would make a person drop everything to go to the one they loved.

She searched the depths of his dark eyes and lost herself. The kiss seemed the most natural thing in the world. Her mouth brushed over his, sending sparks flying. She could feel the struggle going on inside him, him and his darned cowboy code. He was afraid he would end up hurting her.

Kate pulled back, realizing how easy it would be, just the two of them alone in the cabin, to end up doing something they might regret. An image of the two of them beneath one of the thick quilts flashed before her, her lying naked in his arms. She shivered at the thought.

Cyrus hadn't moved. She looked into his eyes

and saw something close to pain. He wanted her as much as she wanted him. But his life was in Denver. Hers was in Whitehorse. This was impossible. And yet it would be so easy to throw caution to the wind.

She knew it would change everything between them. So did he.

"Good night," she mumbled and hurried into one of the bedrooms, closing the door behind her.

CYRUS LISTENED to Kate getting ready for bed in an adjacent room. He groaned, still feeling the effects of her kiss. Damn that woman, she was going to be the death of him. He stood for a long time, staring at her closed door, wanting desperately to go after her, needing her in his arms.

Just the thought of making love to Kate… He moved to the closed bedroom door and pressed his fingers against the cool wood. Listening, he heard nothing beyond the door. Maybe Kate had already fallen asleep.

Or maybe she was lying awake, waiting for him to come to her. He groaned inwardly. He cared too much for her to have casual sex. That thought made him laugh to himself. There would be nothing casual about it.

Growling to himself at the thought, he moved

away from the door to go back to the table. He picked up the stack of letters Kate had found and tried not to think about her, just in the next room in one of those tall iron beds he'd glimpsed through the doorway.

There was one more letter from Katherine to her sister, more urgent than the other one, pleading with Elizabeth to help her.

Cyrus sat down and tried to put Kate out of his mind. But it had been impossible since the day he'd met her.

HOURS LATER, after going through files and boxes filled with every birthday card, Christmas card, note or letter Jenny "Dimple" Landon had ever received in her long life, he found the box with the bank statement in it.

His gaze shot to the return address and he felt his heart drop to his feet. The return address was a bank in Whitehorse.

The statement was under both Katherine Landon's and her mother, Jenny Landon's names. Katherine had apparently had her bank statements sent home to her mother in West Yellowstone.

The statements were filed by date. He pulled out one from the end of December, 1980.

Then he saw the balance and did a double take.

Katherine had deposited five thousand dollars

into a savings account that had previously only had seventeen dollars in it.

Cyrus found the next—and last—statement. Thirty years ago Dimple had closed the savings account and had the money transferred into a local savings account in Kate's name.

As he glanced through the financial papers, he surmised that Dimple had saved the money to make a nice nest egg for her granddaughter.

So that was what Kate had used to buy the old library in Whitehorse and start her shop. He had a feeling that Kate had no idea where the money had come from. Had her grandmother?

He closed the folder, wondering what Dimple had thought when she'd found out that her daughter had put the money in a joint savings account with her as beneficiary. Had she known it might get her killed?

And what had Dimple made of all this? She had to wonder where Katherine had gotten the money. Her daughter had been working as a nurse's aide before assuming a nurse's identity. Still, she hadn't been making much money in Whitehorse.

And suddenly, on Dec. 19, she'd come into five grand. Five thousand dollars on the same day she'd switched the babies in the nursery and gotten herself killed.

Cyrus sighed and turned out the light before

heading to one of the bedrooms Kate had pointed out to him.

The bed had a great iron frame. He climbed up on top of it without even removing his clothes and shut his eyes.

He'd expected his thoughts to be on all the paperwork he'd gone through or the unexplained five grand.

But as he closed his eyes, his only thought was of Kate and the kiss. It hadn't been the first time she'd kissed him. He wanted her. So what was holding him back? Could he really walk away from her when all of this was over?

Hours later, after having trouble getting to sleep, he'd just drifted off when he felt someone touch his shoulder. Cyrus opened his eyes to find Kate standing over him. She was wearing a long white nightgown with what looked like moose on it, but for just an instant he thought she was an apparition straight from his dreams.

"What's wrong?" he asked, sitting up quickly.

She shook her head. "I had a bad dream." She sounded scared and he could see that she was shivering. The temperature had dropped during the night up here at over six thousand feet above sea level.

He reached for the heavy quilt at the end of the bed and she slid in beside him. Covering her, he wrapped an arm around her and pulled her close.

"It was just a bad dream," he whispered into her hair.

"And we all know there is nothing to our dreams."

"Well, you're safe now," he whispered back.

Kate snuggled against him in answer and a few moments later, she was asleep. It took him a lot longer to fall back to sleep with her lying in his arms.

Chapter Ten

Kate woke to the smell of coffee. It was heavenly. She lay in bed for a few moments breathing in the scent before she remembered last night and realized she wasn't in her own bed.

She groaned. She really had to quit kissing Cyrus. She was playing with fire and she knew it. And yet as she climbed into the shower she found herself grinning. Last night she'd had the most wonderful dream while sleeping in his arms.

As she toweled dry and dressed, she remembered the letter she'd found the night before. Now she knew why her mother had left her and gone to Whitehorse. Not that it made it any easier in the daylight.

"Coffee?" Cyrus handed her a mug as she came into the kitchen.

"Am I going to need this?" she asked, seeing the papers he had laid out on the table.

His expression confirmed her fears. She took

a sip of the coffee. It was good. She said as much, then asked, "Okay, what did you find?"

She had to sit down as he told her about the five thousand dollars and how her grandmother had invested it for her.

"That was the money she left me." Her voice broke. "You know where that five thousand came from. Now we know why she switched the babies. Someone paid her to do it."

"Kate, I've had some time to think about this," Cyrus said quickly. "Maybe your aunt did agree to switch the babies and apparently she did take the money, but I believe she got your mother to Whitehorse to talk her out of it. I think you were right about her switching the babies back and that's what got her killed."

She looked into his face. Could she love this man any more? It didn't seem possible, and yet she did. "But she still took the money."

"We know she was already in a bind over her job. For some reason, she hadn't been fired. We also don't know why someone wanted the babies switched. Maybe there was a reason that made it easier for your aunt to go along with the deal," he suggested.

She couldn't help smiling at him. "Thank you."

They both jumped at the knock on the front door of the cabin.

"Kate, it's just me, May," came an elderly female voice.

"It's my grandmother's neighbor and good friend," Kate said to Cyrus before going to answer the door. She hugged May and invited her inside, introducing her to Cyrus.

"Land sakes, what are you two doing?" May said when she spied the mess.

"Going through Grandmother's things," Kate told her and saw the older woman's worried frown. "I know about Aunt Katherine and my mother."

May looked surprised, then wary. "Know what, dear?"

"I know they aren't buried up at Fir Ridge Cemetery. You could save me a lot of trouble by telling me what you know. Please," Kate said, pulling out a chair. "Have a seat."

"I'll get you a cup of coffee," Cyrus suggested.

May looked trapped, but took the chair she was offered. "Oh, dear," she said as Cyrus slid a cup of coffee in front of her. She waved off the offer of sugar and cream. "I don't know that much. Honestly."

"But you know they didn't die the way my grandmother said," Kate prodded.

"Yes." May glanced guiltily at her. "You have to understand. It was such a terrible time for your grandmother. Katherine was always a worry. Elizabeth had just given birth to you. Dimple had seen the letters from Katherine. She tried to talk your mother out of going, but Elizabeth was a strong, confident woman and she loved her sister so much."

"My mother went to help Katherine." Kate had already figured that much out herself. "Did Dimple know what kind of trouble Katherine was in?"

May sighed. "With Katherine it was either money or men. Or both. But Dimple never mentioned exactly what it was. I'm not sure she knew."

"So my mother went. I found a postcard from her to Grandmother saying she was coming home and bringing Katherine with her."

May nodded. "But they never made it."

"Grandmother must have known that something happened to them."

"Of course. That's why she hired the private investigator," May said. She nodded at their surprise. "It wasn't like Dimple to take such a step."

"She didn't call the sheriff?" Cyrus asked.

"No," May said. "She was afraid she would get Katherine in more trouble. Best to handle it privately."

Cyrus glanced at Kate. "And the private investigator?"

"Couldn't find a sign of either of them."

"What about their cars? Those should have turned up," Cyrus said.

May shook her head. "Kate, your mama had taken the bus to see her sister and who knows if Katherine even had a car that ran at that point. When she didn't hear from them, Dimple didn't know what to think. She waited, thinking one or the other or both would turn up. They couldn't have just disappeared."

"She just waited?" Kate asked.

"I remember those days when Elizabeth didn't come home." May took a sip of her coffee. "I saw the change in your grandmother. She knew something had happened to them and it wasn't good. Elizabeth would have moved heaven and earth to get back to you, sweetie," the elderly woman said, patting Kate's hand.

"So she just accepted that they were dead?" Kate demanded.

May bristled at her tone. "Your grandmother had a baby to raise. She did what she had to do for you. Her life became all about protecting you. The last thing she wanted was to have whatever trouble your aunt had gotten into put you in any danger."

"So she came up with the story about

Katherine's weak heart and Elizabeth falling ill with pneumonia," Cyrus said.

"That's right," May said.

"And people believed that?" Kate said.

"Everyone loved your grandmother. If Dimple said the sky was falling, then everyone would have run for cover," May said, clearly in awe of her old friend. "I went to your mother's and aunt's funerals up at Fir Ridge. They were beautiful ceremonies. Everyone in town turned out. After that, your grandmother dedicated her life to you, Kate. She never looked back and neither should you."

Kate looked at Cyrus, frustrated and close to tears. "If only she had contacted the sheriff in Whitehorse right away."

"She knew her daughters were gone the moment she found the bracelet on her doorstep."

"What?" Kate cried.

May looked down at her hands, then back up at Kate. "She found one of the silver bracelets your grandfather made on her doorstep that spring. It was just lying there with one of the bells off lying next to it."

Kate's gaze shot to Cyrus. So the bracelet she had was her aunt's? Just as Cyrus had seen in his dream with the broken bell lying next to it on the nursery floor.

She shot to her feet and rushed into her grandmother's room to her jewelry box. The single bell lay under a nest of costume jewelry. She hadn't noticed it the day she'd found the bracelet—and the postcard that had sent her to Whitehorse.

As she came back into the room, she opened her fist to show Cyrus the tiny sleigh bell lying in her palm.

"When she found the bracelet, she took it as a sign," May said. "You have to understand your grandmother. Dimple Landon was all about living. She was the strongest, most courageous woman I knew, and she did a fine job of raising you. She has always been so proud of you."

"What about justice?" Kate asked. "Wouldn't she have wanted justice?"

May smiled sadly. "I would imagine that she knew justice would be served. All in good time."

ROBERTA WARREN FELT her heart drop as she replaced the phone. The sheriff was coming over to see her. She hadn't asked what it was about. She'd known.

It had started with Kate Landon moving to Whitehorse. The moment Roberta had laid eyes on her, she'd known. The young woman had asked a lot of questions, had even run a photograph in the newspaper.

If you know anything about Katherine or Elizabeth Landon, please call, the ad had said.

Roberta had held her breath, but nothing had come of it. After all, it had been thirty years, and no one knew Elizabeth Landon or would have recognized her from that grainy black-and-white photograph in the ad.

Then Cordell Winchester had called about a murder at the hospital. She'd thought she'd put out that fire, but then his twin, Cyrus, had shown up at the hospital asking not only about the murder and the woman he'd alleged he'd seen in a dream—but about babies in the nursery.

Thirty years ago and now it had all come back to haunt her. Roberta thought of the blood on the nursery floor, the woman lying in it, and felt a shudder of fear move through her. She'd never believed in karma. She didn't want to start now.

But she knew Cyrus Winchester couldn't have dreamed any of this. So where was he getting his information? Who was he getting it from? Someone who wanted to hurt her, the hospital and the town and destroy her career.

Roberta ran a hand through her short hair and tried to still her anger. She'd had a chance to retire and leave this town, but she'd passed it up because she wanted to come to a new, modern hospital for the last years of her career.

She'd made a name for herself in this community despite growing up poor on a dirt farm south of town. Now all of that could be taken away with one fell swoop. She felt all the blood drain from her face at the thought.

Well, she wasn't going down alone. Nor was she going down broke. She'd sworn she would never be poor again.

She reached for the phone, then hesitated. She knew there would be no going back once she made this call.

To hell with that, she thought and, picking up the phone, dialed the local number. "You said not to worry when that woman moved to town, but now this man shows up swearing he saw a woman murdered in the old hospital nursery," she said, keeping her voice down.

"What man?"

"Cyrus Winchester," she said and reached over to turn on her radio. The woman in the next office was a terrible gossip and the walls were thin. Roberta thought maybe she shouldn't have called from here. "He's a *private investigator.* And that isn't all, he's asking about the two babies that were in the nursery the night of the murder."

She heard surprise on the other end of the line.

"He knows. I thought you said—"

"He doesn't know *anything*."

"What if he's found some evidence…"

"I'll take care of it."

"You said that last time." She took a breath. "I'm going to need more money."

Silence, then, "You were already paid."

"You said it was over, that no one would ever know."

"And no one does. I'll take care of this."

"I want more money."

The silence lasted longer this time. "Fine, but don't call me again. I'll contact you." The line disconnected.

Roberta slammed down the phone, her hand shaking. A sliver of worry wedged itself just under her skin like a splinter. She hoped calling hadn't been a mistake.

NOW THAT HE and Kate knew what they were looking for, it didn't take them long to find the canceled check and the report from the private investigator.

Cyrus glanced at the report, then handed it to Kate.

"He came up with nothing?" Just as May had said.

"The P.I. couldn't find your aunt or your mother. Your aunt was going under an assumed name and your mother…" Cyrus shrugged. "With neither of them driving a car, it would have been very hard to track either of them down."

Kate shook her head.

"Unfortunately, the investigation firm she hired in Bozeman has gone out of business. Not that the investigator could help anyway, since he came up empty thirty years ago." Cyrus could see how disappointed she was.

Kate had been quiet since May had left, but somehow she looked more peaceful. Her grandmother had done what she thought was right. Dimple's focus had been on the baby left in her care. And she had done a great job, Cyrus thought. Kate was wonderful.

They dug through more boxes in the attic and some in a shed out back, but they found nothing else of interest.

After breakfast at a diner in West Yellowstone, they drove the ninety miles to Bozeman. On the ride there, Kate was quiet. Cyrus lost himself in his own thoughts.

Main Street Bozeman was bustling, unlike Whitehorse.

"Too much traffic," Kate complained as they

drove through. "I forget how noisy and crazy it is being in a larger town."

Cyrus laughed at that. "You really are a small-town girl at heart. You should come to Denver."

"Maybe I will sometime," she said without looking at him. "By the way, thank you for last night."

"Do you want to talk about your nightmare?"

Kate shook her head. "I don't even remember it."

Cyrus glanced over at her and saw her face. With a jolt, he realized this was the first time she'd ever lied to him.

ROBERTA WARREN LOOKED UP in surprise as the sheriff appeared in her office doorway.

"Do you have a minute?" McCall asked and watched as Roberta glanced at her clean desk as if searching for a reason to be too busy.

After a moment, the hospital administrator rose behind her desk. "Come in."

McCall stepped into the office, closing the door behind her and making Roberta lift a brow.

"Is this official business?" she asked, instantly looking nervous.

McCall took a seat. "I'm here investigating

a nurse who worked at the hospital thirty years ago. Candace Porter?"

Roberta shook her head. "The name doesn't ring a bell." But McCall had already caught her expression. Roberta Warren was a horrible liar.

"Really? She was murdered in your hospital thirty years ago. I would think you would have remembered that name, since I believe she was the only person to be murdered there."

Roberta's cheeks flamed with embarrassment. "I guess I have tried to forget such a tragic incident. And it has been thirty years, as you say."

McCall nodded. "You still have a file on her, though."

The older woman looked as if she might deny it, but seemed to change her mind. "I'm sure we do."

"I'd like to see it. For some reason it wasn't with the police report."

"Now?" Roberta said, clearly caught off guard.

"Now."

"I'm not sure—"

"I'll be happy to help you look for it."

Roberta didn't looked pleased to hear that. "The file would be in our storage facility across town."

McCall got to her feet. "Good thing White-

horse is such a small town. We should be able
to get the file before lunch. Well?" she asked
when the hospital administrator hadn't moved.

"I was just thinking that I would probably
need a judge to—"

"Roberta," the sheriff said patiently, "I can
get a warrant to go through all your records. I'll
just have the storage facility sealed until I get
access. The file should have been in the original
police report. I can't help but wonder why it isn't
in there."

The hospital administrator slowly got to her
feet. Her face was pinched as she reached into
her top drawer, took out a key and opened another drawer in her desk. From there she took
another key, this one on a large key ring. She
straightened.

"I really don't need you to come with—"

"I'm tagging along," McCall said. "Did I mention there is no statute of limitations on murder?
Or the offense for obstructing justice?"

"You don't need to take that tone with me,"
Roberta said, bristling.

"Let me be honest with you," the sheriff said.
"You've made me suspicious enough just in the
last few minutes. If you try to cover anything
up—"

Anger flared in Roberta's eyes, her breath
suddenly ragged. "I most certainly—"

"Let's just get this over with, shall we? Oh, and I'd also like to get the names of the babies that were in the hospital nursery the night Candace Porter was murdered."

All the color washed from the hospital administrator's face. "That will definitely take a subpoena to release that information. Hospital privacy laws—"

"Yes, I'm familiar with those," McCall said, gratified. She didn't have the names, but she did have something she'd come for. Roberta Warren was scared. McCall had been in law enforcement long enough to know what that meant.

The question was, how deeply involved had Roberta been in this mess?

By the time Cyrus drove them through Big Timber, dark clouds hung over the Crazy Mountains. At Harlowton to the north, snowflakes began to fall and by the time they reached Judith Gap, the snow was blowing horizontally and spinning the impressive blades of the wind farm on both sides of the two-lane highway.

"Thirty years ago, five thousand dollars was a lot of money," Kate said when they stopped in Lewistown at a Chinese-food place. They'd both been quiet most of the trip so far, both clearly lost in their own thoughts. "Who in Whitehorse had that kind of money?"

Cyrus shrugged. "There's money there, you

just don't see it like you do in Bozeman or some place where people are moving to Montana and building huge homes. Some of the ranchers do all right, I've heard. They run big spreads. I would imagine any number of them could have raised the five grand."

"I guess we won't know until we get the names of the parents of the babies in the nursery that night," she said with a sigh.

"McCall is working on it. Hopefully, by the time we get home—" His cell phone rang. He smiled. "McCall," he said. "We were just talking about you."

Kate listened to his side of the conversation, filling in the blanks.

"We're on our way back now," Cyrus said. "Lewistown. Sure, we can do that. You'll be at the office? You can't tell me over the phone what you've found out? What about the babies? Yeah, I expected that. Any chance of getting a judge to sign a subpoena? Yeah." He looked over at Kate. "Sure, I understand. Okay, see you in a couple of hours."

"No luck getting the names from the hospital administrator, I take it?" she asked when he hung up.

He shook his head. "But she did say she got Candace Porter's job application. Apparently there isn't much on it. She wants us to stop by."

Kate didn't know what she was feeling. One moment she was depressed, the next hopeful. "We need the names of those babies. There has to be a way."

"We'll get them. Meanwhile, we can check out the application. There might be something there that will help."

She figured if there had been, McCall would have told him about it. But still, now she was anxious to get home as she finished her sesame chicken.

"I just had a thought," Cyrus said and pulled out his phone. "McCall," he said. "I was just wondering. Whitehorse only had one doctor thirty years ago, right? Oh, dead, huh?" He looked disappointed. "Was he also the coroner on the Candace Porter murder case?"

As Cyrus waited he looked across the table at her, a reassuring look on his face. He waited and Kate guessed that McCall was checking.

"What's that?" he asked, sitting up a little straighter. "How about that? No, great, yeah, that is real interestin'." He snapped his phone shut. "Want to guess who the coroner was on the case?"

Kate shook her head, but she couldn't help smiling since Cyrus looked so pleased.

"Roberta Warren, the hospital administrator.

She was filling in because the regular coroner had been hospitalized after an accident."

"How convenient," Kate said.

"My thought exactly."

CYRUS PARKED in front of the sheriff's department. Twilight had settled over the small town. It had taken them longer to drive from Lewistown to Whitehorse than he'd expected because of the snowstorm and all the deer on the highway. Something about the late October day had brought them all out.

McCall was the only one still in the office. She ushered them in, closing the door behind them. Once seated behind her desk, she said, "You were right. The real Candace Porter has been living in Ireland the past thirty years."

"How can we prove that the woman who was murdered was my aunt?" Kate asked.

"The body will have to be exhumed," McCall said.

"She's buried here in town?" Kate asked.

"According to what I've been able to find out, the local mortician donated his services when no next of kin was found."

Cyrus reached over and took Kate's hand. She looked pale, but strong and determined. He hoped once everything was out, this would bring her some relief.

"You said they had been unable to find any next of kin," Cyrus said.

"Apparently the real Candace Porter couldn't be found back then, and, as you can see, there is nothing written on her employment application under *In case of emergency*."

He glanced down the single sheet of paper she handed him, taking in the local address before his gaze lit on the line McCall drew his attention to. He looked closer. There had been a number there, but apparently it had been whited out.

"Wouldn't a hospital especially require an emergency number from an employee?" he asked. "It appears there was a number here but it was covered up," he said, handing the paper to Kate, who looked at it before handing it over to the sheriff.

"I saw that," McCall said. "I'll send it to the crime lab to see if they can recover the number, but I'm betting it was Katherine Landon's mother's number."

"Do we know who hired her?" Cyrus asked.

"Roberta Warren."

He swore under his breath. "If an employee is murdered at the hospital, then wouldn't the next of kin be notified?"

The sheriff nodded. "But apparently your

grandmother was never called because Roberta didn't know who Candace really was."

"But she did know," Kate cried, pulling out the letter they'd found from her aunt to her mother. "Her boss knew she wasn't Candace Porter."

McCall took the letter from her. "Okay, your grandmother was never told, but your mother was in town."

Cyrus nodded. "We think she heard about the murder."

"She would have gone straight to the hospital…" Kate's voice broke.

"Where she would have talked to Roberta."

"Or the sheriff," McCall said. "Okay, what aren't you telling me?"

Cyrus shot Kate a look before he told McCall about the baby switch he'd seen in the dream. "Roberta knew Candace was Katherine. She was her boss. She had to be involved in the baby switch."

"You have no proof Roberta was involved," McCall pointed out. "So far it's all conjecture."

"That's why we have to get the names of those babies," Kate said, sitting forward in her chair. "It's all tied to those babies and why someone hired my aunt to switch them."

McCall lifted a brow. "Hired her?"

Cyrus had brought the paperwork they'd found at Kate's grandmother's cabin. He glanced over at Kate. She nodded and he handed McCall the manila envelope. "Everything we found is in there. It looks like someone paid Katherine Landon, aka Candace Porter, to switch the babies."

"Five thousand dollars?" McCall said as she thumbed through the papers. She stopped on the private investigator's report, her gaze going to Kate. "Your grandmother suspected foul play? But I never saw anything in the file about her contacting the sheriff."

"We suspect she didn't," Kate said. "She hired a private investigator. When he didn't come up with anything…"

"Kate was a baby," Cyrus added. "Her grandmother had her to raise. She symbolically buried her daughters and turned all of her attention to raising Kate."

McCall sat back. "If you're right, someone paid Candace to switch the babies. Why kill her?"

"To cover up the crime," Cyrus said. "Or," he glanced at Kate again, "as Kate has suggested, maybe her mother talked her sister out of it and at the last minute, Katherine switched the babies back and double-crossed the killer."

"You saw all this in your...dream? So now you're saying you could have seen her switching the babies back," McCall said and shook her head. "I can't see Roberta killing anyone in the hospital. The hospital is her little kingdom."

Cyrus agreed. "Roberta is involved, though. She had access to the employment application. She would have been the one to make the call about her murdered employee. Roberta knew Katherine wasn't Candace Porter and yet she didn't fire her. When she found out about Katherine's sister, she would have called someone. She couldn't take the chance that Candace had confided in her sister. Clearly Roberta couldn't trust Candace, since she wasn't even who she said she was and she'd possibly double-crossed whoever was behind the baby switch. Someone would have to take care of the sister quickly."

"Cyrus, we don't know for a fact that when Katherine mentioned in the letter that her boss had found out that she meant Roberta or even that she was telling the truth," McCall pointed out.

He knew he was doing what he'd told Kate not to—jumping to conclusions. "You're right."

"But there is one thing I do know," Kate said, voice breaking. "If my mother had gotten the chance, she would have called my grandmother about Katherine's death. She never got the chance because someone tipped off the killer."

ROBERTA HAD TRIED to talk herself out of it all day. She knew she couldn't chance making the call again from her office. At least not while everyone was around. But she was so shaken by the sheriff's visit.

She'd been told not to call again. What was she supposed to do? Just take all this heat alone?

She grabbed her purse and cell phone and started for the door. Her plan was to go out to her car, pretend to run an errand and make the call so she could be assured that no one would overhear her.

She was almost to the door when she realized that calls made on her cell would show up on the bill. Now more than ever, she had to start covering her tracks.

Closing her office door, she forced herself to go back to her desk. If she called from her office, there could be all kinds of explanations for such a call.

She knew that phone calls were broken down by department and even by office. That was how she kept track of anyone using a phone for personal calls. Her determination to run a tight ship now had it where her line could be monitored, as well.

She had little choice. She couldn't use her cell or her home phone and it would be impossible to find a pay phone in Whitehorse where she knew no one would overhear—or wonder what she was doing.

She'd been forced to wait all day after turning over a copy of Candace Porter's employee file to the sheriff. She flushed at the memory of what the sheriff had said to her. She was a suspect in Candace Porter's murder.

Correct that. Katherine Landon's murder.

And that was only the beginning, Roberta thought. Once the truth came out about that murder, the rest of it would start falling like dominoes.

She checked the clock. Everyone in administration had gone home for the day. All the lights were out but the ones in her office, the hallway dark in this part of the hospital.

Roberta had always loved this time of the day, when she would have the place to herself. She often worked late, so no one had questioned her staying tonight.

She got up and went to her door to look out. She listened for a moment. The only light came from under the double doors that led to the hallway and the nurses' station.

She stepped back into her office, closed the door and picked up the phone with trembling fingers. *Don't call me again. I'll contact you.*

Roberta hesitated, but only for a moment. She shouldn't have to bear the brunt of this alone. She dialed angrily, thinking she would demand more money to keep her mouth shut. She deserved it.

"The sheriff knows," she said without preamble. She hurriedly detailed the sheriff's questions about Candace Porter and the request for not just the employee application but the names of the babies in the nursery.

"You're panicking unnecessarily. They don't know anything and as long as you keep your cool, they never will. I told you, they don't have any evidence. If they did, they would already have a subpoena for the babies' names."

Roberta had heard about the break-in at Second Hand Kate's. Maybe there wasn't any evidence. "But if you'd heard the way the sheriff talked to me… She demanded Candace Porter's file. I had to give it to her. I thought this was over. If it comes out about the babies—"

"Get ahold of yourself. I told you I would take care of everything. You just do your part and relax. This will blow over. Whatever you do, don't call me again." The phone was slammed down.

Roberta replaced her receiver, shaking all

over. She didn't know what upset her the most, the way she'd just been treated or the feeling that her neck alone was on the chopping block. Of course she would be a suspect. She'd been the hospital administrator at the time of the murder. She'd hired Candace Porter.

Her heart began to pound. Everything would come out.

She groaned at the memory of what she'd done—and why. Her reputation would be destroyed. She would deny it all, but she knew it would come down to her word against— With a shock, she realized that *she* was the one who wouldn't be believed. She was the one who would end up in prison.

Her hand went to the phone again. Maybe if she told the sheriff everything…

She pulled back.

It hadn't reached that point yet. She was panicking and it wasn't like her.

Roberta straightened her skirt, brushed a piece of lint from the sleeve of her jacket and tried to calm down.

They didn't know anything. They wouldn't find anything. The worst that could happen was that the truth might come out about who Candace Porter was.

Roberta told herself that she would pretend to be as shocked about that news as anyone. She would weather this storm and in a few months she would retire and take her money and move to someplace warm, far from Whitehorse, Montana.

But, she thought, she was going to need a lot more money for being forced to go through this alone. And she would damn sure call when the time came.

Chapter Eleven

"I know it's a long shot," Cyrus said as they left the sheriff's department. "But I thought we should check out the address your aunt put on her employment application."

Kate had been thinking the same thing. She felt a little shell-shocked after everything they'd found out. She hugged herself. It had gotten dark while they were inside. The wind had come up and now kicked up dust from the street. There was a chill in the air as she climbed into Cyrus's pickup and they drove the four blocks across town.

The apartment house was large and rambling, once an old farmhouse that had sat alone before the town encroached on it. As they walked to the door, piles of dried fallen leaves blew around their feet.

Inside the front door was a list of names of people who lived there. Most of the slots were empty. Apartment three was marked "manager" and the name Harkin.

At Cyrus's knock, an elderly gentleman with a shock of white hair and a small wrinkled face like one of those apple dolls answered.

"Hello, Mr. Harkin?" Kate asked. "We'd like to talk to you about one of your renters."

"Candace Porter." He laughed at her surprise. "The sheriff called earlier." He opened the door wider. "Come on in. And call me Harry. Everyone does."

"The sheriff already called?" Cyrus asked.

"Wanted to know if I remember renting to the woman. I said, 'What do you think, that I'm losing my mind?' Ha, I'm as sharp as a tack." He smiled and ushered them in, winking at both her and Cyrus.

Once inside, the old man eyed Kate, then Cyrus. "Newlyweds? I've got a nice two-bedroom on the second floor."

"We're not looking for an apartment," Cyrus said. "Kate owns Second Hand Kate's downtown and lives over the shop. I'm just here visiting from Colorado."

That about sized it up, Kate thought. Once this was over Cyrus would be going back to his life in Colorado. She knew she'd needed that reminder, but it still depressed her. She was going to miss him terribly. She'd come to depend on Cyrus and that, she realized, was a mistake.

Was there a woman waiting for him back in Denver? If that was true, wouldn't the woman have come to Montana with him? Kate would have. She wouldn't have let him come up here alone, not when he'd just come out of a coma.

"So you remember Candace Porter living here thirty years ago?" Cyrus asked.

"Sure do. She was a looker," Harkin said and grinned over at Kate. "Kinda looked like you, now that I think about it."

"I'm Candace's niece."

"Oh." He sobered. "Sorry. What would you like to know?"

"Anything you can tell us," Kate said.

"I'll tell you what I told the sheriff. Candace lived here for four months."

"You can remember that after thirty years?" Cyrus asked, sounding skeptical.

"I'm good, but I'm not that good," Harkin said with a laugh. "I looked up her file. I keep files on all my renters. But I remember Candace. She was a loner. She just went to work, worked nights, and never made any noise. I felt kind of sorry for her. If I'd been younger…" He let the thought die off. "I was shocked when she was murdered."

"Did the sheriff question you about the murder at the time?" Cyrus asked.

"Sure did. I told him what I told you. He looked through her apartment. She didn't have much and that was that. Never did catch the bastard. Excuse my language," he said to Kate. "I just made some coffee. Sit down." He disappeared into the kitchen before they could decline his offer.

Kate shrugged and they looked around for a place to sit.

The apartment was filled from top to bottom. No flat surface wasn't covered. Under the scent of fresh-perked coffee was dust, mildew and old age.

Cyrus made a place for them to sit on the old chesterfield couch as Harkin returned with a small tray and three cups filled with coffee. He shoved a stack of newspapers to the floor and set down the tray on a corner of the coffee table.

"Don't get many visitors. Live alone since the wife died," he said.

Cyrus handed Kate a cup of coffee, then took one for himself. Kate took a tentative sip. The coffee was strong and bitter.

"I'm surprised you keep records that long," Cyrus said.

"Got records from longer back than that," Harkin said with a laugh and pointed to a small alcove. It was filled with filing cabinets, an assortment of papers piled high on top of each.

He put down his coffee to go into the alcove and open one of the filing cabinets. Amazingly he, came out with a folder. "Candace Porter." He smiled and tapped the discolored folder with his finger before handing it to Cyrus.

He opened it so Kate could see. The application for the apartment was sketchy at best, most of the lines left empty. Her aunt had paid one hundred and forty dollars a month with a fifty-dollar cleaning deposit. She'd apparently stayed just over four months.

"What did you do with her belongings?" Kate asked, even though she was sure that he'd tossed them out or the sheriff had taken them.

The old man pointed at the file folder. "Says right in there at the bottom of the application that if anyone leaves anything it will be held for thirty days, then discarded or sold at my discretion."

"So whatever she left is gone." Kate couldn't hide her disappointment. Thirty years was a long time and she'd guess this place had been through a lot of renters and their leftover stuff in that time.

"Actually, there wasn't enough to worry about. I just boxed it up and forgot about it. When the sheriff called, I told her I was sure I'd gotten rid of the box. But then I got to thinking…." He got up and went to a box sitting just inside the door, which Kate hadn't noticed until now. "I got it out of my shed out back."

Printed on the side of the box were the name *C. Porter* and the date: Dec. 24, 1980. He set it down in front of them on the floor.

"I figured her sister might have wanted what she left behind," Harkin said.

"Sister?" Kate said, her voice breaking.

"Her sister was here visiting her. Only visitor I ever saw her have except for that other nurse, now that I think about it. Sarah. Sarah Welch Barnes now. I heard she's visiting her sister down in Old Town." He seemed to shake himself. "Where was I? Oh, her sister. She was staying here but left after… I thought she'd come by for Candace's things, but she never did. I'm afraid that's all she left behind," he said in conclusion.

They thanked him, promised to stop by sometime and left. Cyrus put the box in the back of the truck as Kate climbed in. As Cyrus joined her, his cell phone rang.

Cyrus was surprised to see that the call was from his grandmother. He shouldn't have been. Whitehorse was a small town. Of course she would have heard that he was back and out of his coma. He felt guilty for not calling her.

"I was hoping you'd come out to the ranch," Pepper Winchester said. "I would love to see you. Bring your friend."

"My friend?" he asked as he glanced over at Kate.

A slight chuckle, then, "Kate Landon. You didn't really think I hadn't heard about the two of you, did you? My ranch is remote. It's not on another planet. Maybe you could come out for dinner. Your aunt Virginia is here."

Aunt Virginia. He remembered her only too well as being mean when he was boy.

"Tomorrow would be good. I'll have Enid make something special."

He was still amazed that his grandmother's housekeeper and cook was still alive. "I'll have to get back to you on that."

"I really do need to see you, Cyrus."

He felt a stab of guilt. Three months ago he'd been on his way to see her before he'd been put into a coma. "All right."

"Bring Kate." It sounded like an order as she hung up.

"That was my grandmother," Cyrus said, snapping his phone shut. "She wants us to come out to dinner. Tomorrow night."

"Us?" Kate asked in surprise.

"Apparently the Whitehorse grapevine is in fine working order. Do you mind?"

"No, I told you I've been wanting to meet her." She smiled over at him. "I've kept you from seeing her and I'm sorry. My problems have taken over your life."

He shook his head. "You've been the best thing about all this."

THE WELCH RANCH was outside of Old Town Whitehorse, the original settlement back when Whitehorse had been nearer to the Missouri River. But when the railroad came through, the town migrated ten miles north, taking the name with it. Old Town Whitehorse was now little more than a ghost town, except for a handful of ranches and a few of the original buildings.

A woman in her sixties opened the door, wearing an apron and a smile. Kate could hear country-western music playing in the background and the scent of chocolate-chip cookies baking wafted out the open door into the crisp fall air.

"We're looking for Sarah Welch Barnes," Cyrus said.

"You've found her and you're just in time," she said. "The cookies are still warm." She ushered them into the kitchen and introduced the slightly older woman scooping dough onto a baking sheet as her sister Mary. "What would you like to drink? I have some apple cider." She looked at each of them, smiling, as she opened the refrigerator and took out a gallon jug of cider. "This came from our trees."

"Sarah, we're here about someone you used to work with at the hospital," Cyrus said. "I'm—"

"I know. You're Cyrus, a private investigator from Denver, and you're Kate, you own a shop in Whitehorse that everyone is talking about." She smiled. "Agnes Palmer stopped by this morning. She *sees* things. She told me you would be stopping by so I told Mary we should bake some cookies." She handed each of them a glass of cider. "Sit. Help yourself to some cookies." She motioned to the cookies cooling on the racks on the table. "I'm not sure what I can tell you about Candace, though."

Kate shot Cyrus a glance. "I'm sorry, you said a woman told you we would be stopping by?"

"Agnes Palmer. It's the darnedest thing," Mary said. "She's psychic. Seriously, she just knows things. I don't think she likes it, but she says it must be God's will since it all started last year when she was struck by lightning out in her garden trying to save her tomatoes. She grows the most beautiful tomatoes." Sarah smiled. "But you want to know about your aunt."

As Kate sat down at the table, she realized she hadn't mentioned Candace was her aunt.

"I liked Candace. I befriended her, I guess you would say. I felt a little sorry for her. She just seemed so…lost." She slid a rack of cookies toward them as Cyrus pulled out a chair and joined Kate. "You really should try them while they are still warm."

Kate took a cookie, as did Cyrus. "What do you mean…lost?"

"I just had a feeling that she'd had a hard life. We weren't close friends. I worked her shift sometimes for her when she didn't feel well."

"Was she ill?" Kate asked, alarmed.

"More like depressed. I got the feeling that she'd struggled. I know she didn't have much money. She didn't own a car and the one time I stopped by her apartment, it was clear she didn't have much."

"Any idea who might have wanted to harm her?" Cyrus asked.

Sarah shook her head. "And it's sad because I had the feeling that her life was just starting to turn around. She just seemed…happier."

Kate wondered if that had to do with Elizabeth being there.

"She was even dating."

"Dating?" Cyrus asked.

"Well, I should say, she'd been out a couple of times."

"Do you know who the man was?" Kate asked.

"Audie. Audie Dennison. They met at the hospital." She smiled. "Audie is the nicest man you'd ever want to meet. His older sister Marie raised him after their parents died. She's a lot older than Audie." She sobered. "I heard she isn't well. I'm sure Audie is looking after her the way she looked after him when they were kids."

"Was he a patient when he met Candace?" Cyrus asked.

"No, his sister, Marie, was. She had a rough pregnancy because of her age, so she was in the hospital for the last few weeks before her son was born."

Kate shot Cyrus a look.

"She gave birth to a son?"

Sarah smiled. "Jace. A beautiful boy."

Cyrus took a cookie. "Was Jace born before Candace was killed?" He took a bite of the cookie. "Umm, these are wonderful."

Sarah beamed. "Thank you. Jace was born that night. I remember because it was just crazy around the hospital. Marie had some complications. We were all so afraid all during her pregnancy that she would lose the baby. Then in the labor room, the baby was breech." Her smiled brightened. "But he turned and was finally born. Well, it was nothing but a miracle, since Marie never thought she'd have a baby and she'd wanted one so badly. She would have done anything to have a baby and then to have Jace…"

"Was that the only baby born that night?" Cyrus asked.

Sarah laughed. "No, that was what made that night so crazy. The other mother in labor was… well, she was a screamer, demanding, nothing like Marie, and what made it so hard was that she gave birth within minutes of Marie. We really could have used more help."

"Do you remember the name of the other mother?" Kate asked.

Sarah rolled her eyes. "I sure do. I still feel guilty about it because I gave her to your aunt, who ended up delivering the baby since the doctor was busy with Marie. I think it was Candace's first birthing. I remember the way she looked at that baby boy. It was heartbreaking. I really think she would have liked a baby of her own and maybe she would have had one with Audie, if things had been different."

"You said you remember the name of the woman who gave birth to the second boy that day?" Cyrus asked again.

Sarah hesitated. "Agnes warned me it had to do with the night Candace was killed and those two babies. I suppose it's all right to tell you. After all, it's been thirty years. I mean, this can't be about a lawsuit, because I can tell you that Candace did nothing wrong. That baby was as healthy as could be when he was born."

"Are you saying the second baby died?" Kate asked, her heart in her throat.

"I thought you knew," Sarah said, looking confused. "Sudden infant death. We still don't know what causes it. There wasn't an autopsy done, but maybe the baby had a weak heart. With all the confusion, the doctor didn't get to take a good look at the babies before Candace took them down to the nursery."

Kate couldn't speak. Had her aunt known that the baby wasn't well? Is that why she'd agreed to switch the babies?

"Sarah," Cyrus said. "We're just trying to find out who killed Candace and why."

"I am sorry, dear."

"Thank you," Kate said. "I was wondering. Did Candace ever wear a silver bracelet?"

"With tiny bells on it," the woman said, brightening. "Wore it all the time. The patients loved it. That little tinkling sound. They could always tell when she was around. Oh, I am so glad this isn't about Virginia. It would be just like her to be looking for someone to blame for the death of her baby, even after all these years."

"Virginia?" Cyrus said and Kate heard something break in his voice.

"Virginia Winchester." Sarah must have seen his expression. "She had the other baby that night. Do you know her?"

"VIRGINIA WINCHESTER IS MY AUNT," Cyrus told Kate the moment they were in his pickup headed back to town.

"Did you know she had a baby?"

"No. As far as I know she was never married or even dated, for that matter."

"That's terrible about the baby dying," Kate said. "But what if the baby that wasn't well was the other woman's and my aunt knew it?"

Cyrus had thought of that. Given what Sarah Barnes had said about Marie Dennison, her advanced age, her desire for a baby and the problems she had giving birth, he could see how anyone would want to see her leave the hospital with a healthy baby boy—especially if Virginia was unwed and, well, Virginia. She had a way of rubbing people the wrong way.

She'd certainly made a negative impression on Sarah Welch. He could well imagine she hadn't been popular with Candace, either. For all he knew, Virginia could have been planning to give the baby up, which would have made it even easier for Kate's aunt to agree to switch the babies.

"Do you think Jace Dennison is your cousin?" Kate asked.

"I have no idea. I've never seen him. We left here when I was seven, and as far as I know my family didn't even know the Dennisons."

He'd never imagined that this would hit so close to home. But given that he'd dreamed it while in a coma, he knew he shouldn't have been surprised.

"What are you going to do?" Kate asked.

Cyrus looked over at her. Her concern touched him. "I'm going to make sure you're safe. Do you mind if we swing by my hotel and pick up the rest of my things? I'd like to stay with you at the shop."

She nodded and he quickly added, "I thought I could sleep in one of those bedrooms you have made up in the shop, if that's okay."

"Sure. Thank you. I have to admit I feel a little spooked knowing there is a killer still out there."

She wasn't the only one.

Cyrus ran into the hotel, leaving the truck running and Kate waiting. It only took him a few moments to get the rest of his belongings. He wondered why he hadn't checked out before they went to West Yellowstone. Hadn't he known he was going to stay with Kate until this was over?

In his room, he noticed something he hadn't before. The place had been searched—just as Kate's place had been gone through. He'd had so little to search, he hadn't paid any attention when he'd stopped by here on the way to West Yellowstone.

As far as he could tell, nothing had been taken because, he suspected, the intruder hadn't found what he or she had been looking for.

He made an inquiry at the desk, but of course he was told that no one had asked for him and no one had let anyone into his room.

But clearly someone was worried that he and Kate knew more than they did.

KATE HADN'T BEEN able to hide her relief when Cyrus asked to stay with her. She really hadn't been looking forward to spending the night alone—not after the nightmare she'd had last night.

She'd told Cyrus she didn't remember it. She hadn't wanted to worry him. But she did: in the dream, someone had tried to kill her. She feared telling Cyrus about the dream would only make him more determined to keep her out of this investigation.

Once they reached her shop and apartment, Cyrus had checked to make sure no one had been there. He'd changed the locks before they'd left, but he said he wanted to make sure there hadn't been another break-in.

There hadn't.

"I need to check the basement," he said.

"Thanks." She could tell he was upset about what they'd learned and probably just wanted to keep busy. That and he wanted to keep his distance from her.

"Would you mind fixing that cable down there?" she asked. "Halloween is day after tomorrow and the haunted house opens at five o'clock, right after I close the shop."

He looked like he might argue that she should cancel the haunted house. She didn't give him a chance and hurried off to get a shower. From upstairs she could hear him working. It was a comforting sound.

She'd always felt she could take care of herself. Now, though, she felt uneasy. Knowing there was a killer still on the loose—a killer who she feared had been in her shop and apartment—had her feeling vulnerable. She hated the feeling and was determined to go back to loving this place and her life here.

But even as she thought it, Kate knew that it was more than just catching the killer and finding out the truth. It was Cyrus. This place would never feel the same once he was gone.

It was late by the time he finished. Cyrus showered while she made them a snack. She wore a skirt, knit top and ballet shoes, and it felt good to be home, especially with him here.

"I baked cupcakes," she said when he came out of the bathroom. "But if you're hungrier than that, I could make us an omelet." He smelled heavenly and his damp hair curled at the nape of his neck.

She hardly ever saw him when he wasn't wearing his Stetson. She'd thought he couldn't look any sexier than in it, but she'd been wrong.

Standing there, freshly showered in a T-shirt and jeans, he was the sexiest man she'd ever seen. He looked almost shy as he thanked her, but passed, saying he wasn't hungry.

"Are you afraid of my cooking?" she asked, only half joking. She had a pretty good idea that it wasn't the cupcakes he was passing on. She sensed he was anxious to call it a night.

She tried to hide her disappointment. She'd hoped they would sit around and talk for a while.

"Kate—"

"Not to worry. The cupcakes will keep until tomorrow."

"I'm leaving after this is over."

His words hit her hard, even though she'd been expecting them. "I know."

"I can't leave my brother to take care of our business forever," he said.

"No, of course not. I realize that I've kept you from your work in Denver, your life—"

"That's not what I'm talking about," he said, taking a step toward her. "Kate," he said taking her shoulders in his hands.

"Thank you for staying as long as you have," she said quickly, afraid of what he was going to say.

"I care about you," he said, his voice rough. "Too much. Being with you…" He shook his head and let go of her. "I can't do this."

She told herself this would be worse if they'd made love and felt her eyes burn with tears from the lie. "It's late," she said pointedly and started to step past him.

Cyrus grabbed her arm, stopping her.

Desire spread through her, centering at her core, making her ache for him. "Please," she said, pleading, but not for what he thought.

He quickly let go of her. "I'll see you in the morning." He strode out of the room and down the stairs.

She stood, fighting the need to call him back, knowing how much harder it would be for him if she did.

IT WAS DARK by the time Roberta reached her house. She'd bought a place up on the hill overlooking Whitehorse. It was the part of Whitehorse people moved up to when they had enough money.

The way the house was situated she had a lot of privacy, something else she liked. She'd planted a hedge along each side and trees formed a shelter at the front and back.

She knew her neighbors, but she made a point of not being too friendly. When she came home, she wanted to be alone and unwind.

Roberta knew that people in town talked about her. The problem with Whitehorse was that everyone knew your business and most people had been around long enough to know everything about you from the time you were that poor little Roberta Thompson.

Marrying Mark Warren had been the smartest thing she'd ever done. He had been sixteen years older. She'd married him for his money and for what he could give her and he'd never tried to renege on their agreement. She liked being married in name only, liked being Mrs. Roberta Warren.

She'd wanted an education. He'd seen that she got it. What she hadn't told him was that she planned to leave Whitehorse in the dust once she was finished with her schooling.

But it hadn't turned out that way. Mark had gotten sick and she had to come back to take care of him. She'd gone to work at the hospital when she'd found out that her husband didn't have any money and had mortgaged the ranch to the hilt to pay the bills. He had a gambling habit she hadn't known about and had borrowed against the ranch.

Now, as she pulled up into her driveway and turned off the engine and lights, Roberta recalled that awful feeling in the pit of her stomach the day she'd learned that Mark was broke. *They* were broke.

Fortunately, she'd had her job at the hospital. But his medical bills in the years before he died had kept her from leaving Whitehorse.

"Water under the bridge," she said to herself and was startled how much she sounded like her mother. But unlike her mother, she had a plan. Soon she would leave and see the world.

Opening her car door, she grabbed her purse and stepped out. As the dome light went out in her car, she realized just how dark it was.

Wind whirled the fallen leaves around the bottom of the trees in the front yard. She'd heard a storm was blowing in. Always did this time of year.

Roberta caught movement out of the corner of

her eye and froze. Was that someone standing alongside the hedge by the garage?

She stared until her eyes ached but saw nothing. Just her imagination. But she still stood listening, though, her skin prickling with unease even as she told herself she was just being silly. There was no one there.

Relieved and feeling foolish, she hurried forward through the breezeway toward the side door. It was even darker back here. She wished she'd remembered to leave the outside lights on. But then she hadn't known she was going to be this late when she'd left that morning.

She fumbled with her key, suddenly nervous again. Her imagination seemed to be going wild. She felt as if someone was standing right behind—

A hand dropped onto her shoulder. She jumped, letting out a cry and spun around, her heart in her throat. Relief washed over her. "Oh, it's just you. What are you doing here?"

Chapter Twelve

Cyrus mentally kicked himself as he went downstairs. What the hell was wrong with him? He wanted Kate, that's what was wrong with him. Then why was he holding back?

Because he was going to have to leave here soon. He had to get back to his business. He couldn't leave Cordell handling all of it alone.

But just the thought of leaving Kate was killing him.

He knew that if he made love with her, he would never get over her. He wasn't even sure he would now.

Cyrus thought he would never get to sleep, his body aching for the woman lying upstairs and his mind awhirl with Kate and this case.

He woke to the clamor of footfalls on the stairs. He shot up in bed as Kate came running into the room. One look at her face and his pulse took off.

"What is it?" he cried, leaping from the bed.

He'd gone to sleep as he had in West Yellow-stone, wearing only his jeans.

Her green eyes were huge with fear and she was shaking. "Didn't you hear it?"

All he'd heard was her coming down the stairs. Was someone breaking in again? He looked past her, uncomprehending, and reached for the gun hanging in his shoulder holster next to the bed.

Then he heard it.

A chill rippled over his flesh and his heart began to pound, his mouth going dry.

Somewhere close by there was the sound of a baby crying.

"What the hell?" he said under his breath as another chill snaked up his spine. He stepped past her following the sound, Kate at his heels.

Outside the trees thrashed in the wind. A storm had blown in during the night. Shadows played on the old hardwood floors. He moved through them as the wail of the crying baby filled the old building.

The baby quit crying.

He stopped. He could hear his heart pounding and feel Kate gripping his free hand. There was nothing but the wind at the windowpanes.

The crying started up again. Cyrus realized

where the sound was coming from. The display room Kate had decorated as a baby's nursery.

At the doorway, he looked in. Faint light bled through the window from the streetlamp outside. He could see the crib. It was full of dolls of all sizes and colors. He snapped on the overhead light and stared into the mass of tiny faces, looking for the real baby.

Kate let go of his hand and stepped to the crib. She leaned over and picked up one. It stopped crying as she turned with it in her arms. "It's just a doll," she said, her relief audible.

Something fell from the doll to the floor. A scrap of paper. Cyrus reached for it, sure that whoever had left it hadn't left fingerprints. Still, he was careful to pick it up by the edge. The handwriting was the same as the other note Kate had received. Written in childish scrawl were the words *Don't make me warn you again.*

The baby doll began to cry again.

Cyrus dropped the note into the crib and took the doll from her arms. "It's remote-controlled," he said as he found the batteries at the doll's back and dumped them into the crib as well.

The doll stopped crying. The room fell eerily silent.

He laid the doll back into the crib and looked at Kate. She wore a long white-cotton nightgown. Her hair was loose and hung around her shoulders in a rich wave of copper. Her eyes, so wide and beautiful, looked even greener than he remembered. The desire came like a punch to the chest.

"I should make some hot chocolate," she said and started to step away.

This time when he touched her, he felt her quiver as if an electrical current had run through her body.

"No hot chocolate," he said, his voice sounding hoarse even to him. He told himself all the reasons that this was a mistake as he pulled her to him, his mouth dropping to hers. She emitted a small cry of pleasure as he drew her closer, deepening the kiss.

He'd never wanted anyone as much as he wanted Kate. All thought left him as he felt her full breasts press against his bare chest, felt his heart take off like a wild stallion. He swept her up into his arms and carried her back to his room.

As he gently set her down on the bed, she looped her arms around his neck, her gaze locking with his. He looked into her beautiful emerald eyes and was lost.

KATE'S SKIN FELT ALIVE, her heart a thunder in her chest, her pulse thrumming in her ears as she looked into Cyrus's dark eyes.

"Kate, oh, Kate," he whispered, his voice hoarse with the desire she saw in the dark depths of his gaze.

She smiled as she felt him surrender to it. They'd been racing toward this moment from that first day they'd met. Cyrus slowly began to unbutton the front of her gown, his expression daring her to stop him.

His fingertips brushed the tender flesh of her breast, making her shiver with expectation. He kissed her, cupping one full breast in the palm of his hand, then trailed kisses from her neck down to the slope of her breast to the rock-hard nipple.

She arched into him, her palms against his hard chest. Her fingers followed the dark line of hair from his chest to the V at the top of his jeans. She worked at the buttons, freeing him of the rest of his clothing.

He stood over her for a moment, just looking down at her. His gaze made her feel like the most beautiful woman in the world.

As he pulled the nightgown up over her head, she drew him to her, desperately needing to feel his naked flesh against hers.

Their lovemaking became a blur of caresses and kisses, his hot mouth on hers before moving down her body, leaving a trail of fire over aching nipples to her center. With the wind howling outside, they were enveloped in a storm of their own.

When Cyrus entered her, she cried out and gripped the iron headboard, her body glazed with sweat, her heart swelling as he took her with him to the peak of pleasure.

Later, lying in each other's arms, they heard the wind die down and looked out to see that it was snowing. Huge, lacy flakes drifted down to make the world outside into a fairyland of white.

They made love again, slowly, tenderly, and then slept, wrapped in each other's arms. It was there that Kate woke hours later.

CYRUS CAME AWAKE SLOWLY, as if from a dream. At first he thought it was daylight out, the snow was so bright. But when he looked at the clock he saw that it was only a little after three in the morning.

He realized at once what had woken him.

Kate was gone.

He sat up, listening for her, then quickly threw his legs over the side of the bed to pull on his jeans. Padding barefoot across the wood floor, he heard a sound coming from upstairs and smelled hot chocolate.

As he topped the stairs, he saw her sitting in the middle of the floor wearing a pink chenille robe. She had a cup of hot chocolate next to her and the box from her aunt's apartment in front of her. He watched her cut the tape on the box with a paring knife, then hesitate.

She saw him then and smiled. "I woke up and couldn't get back to sleep. There's extra hot chocolate." She motioned toward the stove.

He smiled, kissing her on the top of her head as he went to the stove to pour himself a cup. He dropped three large marshmallows into the cup on his way back to her.

Kate hadn't moved.

"You don't have to open the box," he said, seeing her hesitation.

"Yes, I do," Kate said. She grabbed the cardboard flaps and pulled them apart. He watched her, thinking how strong and determined she was. Thinking also that he had fallen for this remarkable woman.

He got a glimpse of the contents of the box. Clothes, just as he'd thought. She pulled out one item of clothing after another, tossing them aside. At the bottom of the box were a few toiletries. She held up the hairbrush.

With a jolt, he saw that there was still hair in the brush. "Kate—"

"DNA," she said with a knowing nod as she handed him the brush.

Suddenly she seemed to freeze before reaching

into the box again. She brought out what he recognized at once as a small address book.

Her gaze swung up to meet his, then she opened the book and quickly leafed through the pages.

Even from where he was sitting he could see that the address book was nearly empty.

He saw her disappointment as she handed it to him. Starting at the As he went through each page. Under D was Dimple's name and phone number and a post office box in West Yellowstone.

He found a Sarah with a Whitehorse number. Sarah Welch, he figured. There was also a number for the hospital. Under Harkin was a number, the same one as the apartment house where Katherine had lived.

Cyrus stopped on the Js, sensing a change in Kate. He looked up to see her flipping through a handful of photographs. She stilled on the last one, tears filling her green eyes. "Kate?"

Soundlessly she handed him a photograph of her mother and aunt. They were standing outside next to a huge old pine. He recognized the tree as the one in front of the Whitehorse apartment house where Katherine had been living as Candace Porter. There was snow on the ground, and both women wore coats and gloves, but their heads were uncovered. Katherine's hair was pulled up in a ponytail. Elizabeth's was down around her shoulders.

They were both smiling at the camera, but the smiles didn't seem to reach their eyes.

He glanced at the date stamped on the back of the photograph: December 18, 1980. The day before Katherine was murdered.

"It proves my mother was here just the day before," Kate said.

"The sheriff will want to see this. Did you find anything interesting in the other photographs?"

Kate picked them up from her lap and handed them to him.

There were several of Katherine in her nurse's aide uniform at the hospital. One with another nurse, a much younger Sarah Welch.

As Kate began to put everything back into the box, he went through the rest of the address book. But there were no more names under the alphabetized sections.

Cyrus was about to close the book when he saw a phone number written small and in pencil at the very back of the book. The number had a local prefix, but no name.

He frowned, realizing it looked familiar. Curious, he took out his cell phone and dialed it.

After four rings, an elderly voice picked up.

The moment he recognized the voice he realized why the number had been so familiar.

Still, he had to ask. "Who is this?"

"You've reached Winchester Ranch. Who were you calling?"

He hung up and looked over at Kate who was watching him now with interest. His mind spun like a top. Why would Katherine Landon have his grandmother's number?

KATE COULDN'T HELP but feel anxious about meeting Cyrus's grandmother, especially after he'd found her number in Aunt Katherine's address book.

"Why would your grandmother be involved in this?" she asked when they stopped by the sheriff's department to tell McCall what they'd learned from Sarah Welch—and Katherine's address book.

Both McCall and Cyrus had laughed.

"Pepper Winchester manipulate one of her children's lives?" Cyrus said with a groan. "You have no idea."

"Our grandmother always has an agenda," McCall said.

"But aren't you having your wedding out there at Christmas?" Kate asked.

"She caught me at a weak moment," the sheriff said. "Don't think I'm not worried. But my fiancé, Luke, assures me it will be fine no matter what."

"I just can't believe a mother would have any part of switching her own daughter's baby with another one and letting her daughter believe all these years that her son died," Kate said.

"I'm sure Pepper had her reasons," Cyrus said and looked to McCall, who shrugged.

"I never knew Virginia had a baby," McCall said. "They must have kept it pretty hush-hush. Any idea who the father of the baby might have been?"

"I was only four at the time," Cyrus said. "It was news to me. But we're having dinner at Grandmother's tonight. I intend to ask her."

McCall raised a brow. "Grandmother invited me, as well. I was planning to go, but now…" she joked. "Truthfully, the crying doll, the notes, that isn't the way our grandmother operates. She's much more direct."

"Well, between the two of us tonight, maybe we can get the truth out of her," Cyrus said as they rose to leave.

"Thanks for the information about the babies," McCall said. "I put in a call to Roberta Warren, but apparently she called in sick." The sheriff smiled and nodded. "I'm sure she's avoiding me. I'll try to get hold of Jace Dennison. We'll need a DNA test to clear this up. I'm hoping he'll cooperate. His mother is real sick, I heard. He is probably headed home. I'm sure his uncle, Audie, let him know. That's interesting that Candace Porter, aka Katherine Landon, dated him."

"You think he talked her into switching the babies when she told him that his sister's baby wasn't well?" Kate asked.

"Or maybe the deal was already planned," Cyrus said. "Katherine could have confided in him, not about the money part. They could have both believed that Marie deserved the healthy baby. Virginia wasn't married and wasn't likeable."

"She was also young," McCall said. "She could have had more babies, while it sounds as if this was Marie's last chance. If Katherine changed her mind... Well, Audie idolized his older sister. Everyone's always said he would do anything for her."

"Even kill?" Cyrus asked.

McCall shrugged. "I guess we'll find out."

JUST AFTER LUNCH, McCall drove out to the Dennison place, a small, old homestead and ranch north of town. Audie lived in the old homestead house up the road from his sister and pretty much ran the small ranch they had shared since Jace left.

On this chilly fall day, McCall found him out behind the house chopping wood. He swung the axe, bringing it down on a log, wood chips flying into the air, as she walked over to him.

He stopped, breathing hard and looked at her. McCall feared that the rumors in the town had reached him. Any talk of the woman he'd dated would have him wary if he had any part in her murder.

"Sheriff," he said and set another log on the chopping block.

She stepped back as he brought the axe down. Half the log flew off in her direction. She side-stepped it, the chunk barely missing her leg.

"Need a moment of your time," she said.

"Yeah?"

He started to pick up another log to split.

"We can talk here or down at my office," she said. In truth, he didn't have to talk to her at all and she suspected he knew it.

She'd never liked Audie. He was a short, stocky man with an attitude problem, one of those men who seemed to think he'd gotten short shrift in life and wasn't happy about it.

In his late fifties, he was still physically fit. He'd never married and the only person he seemed to give a damn about was his sister. Only when he was around Marie and Jace did he soften enough to be almost likeable.

"What's it going to be, Audie?" McCall asked. "You have a permit for that wood you cut up in the Little Rockies?"

"You can't prove that's where I got it."

"But it would give me the right to take you in for questioning."

He slowly put down the axe and crossed his arms over his barrel chest.

"I'm sure you've heard I'm looking into Candace Porter's murder." When he said nothing, she added, "She was the nurse who was—"

"I remember Candace."

"You dated her, I understand."

"We went out a few times."

"What was she like?"

He shrugged. "Quiet."

"I'm going to cut to the chase, Audie. I have reason to believe she might have been paid to switch your sister's baby with the Winchester baby."

He let out a colorful curse. "Who the hell came up with that? That guy from Colorado *dream* that?"

McCall felt something give inside her at his response. It felt rehearsed and without the kind of fury she would have expected. "So you're saying there's no chance that happened?"

His gaze narrowed as he took a step toward

her. "Jace is Marie's son and I won't have you—"

"Easy," she said, her hand slipping to her sidearm.

He stopped moving toward her. "You want to know who killed Candace? Why don't you ask your grandmother? That's right. She didn't want her daughter having that baby."

"Why is that?" McCall asked, even though she knew her grandmother would have had her reasons.

"Are you serious? Don't you know who that baby's daddy was?" He let out a bark of a laugh. "And you're the sheriff?"

"Who was the father?" she asked, disliking Audie all the more.

"Jordan McCormick."

She studied him, trying to decide if he was telling the truth or not, her heart pounding. Her grandmother would have been livid at even the thought of Virginia with Jordan McCormick. There'd been a feud between the two ranching families as far back as she could remember. Rumor had it the feud started when Pepper Winchester had an affair with Joanna McCormick's husband, Hunt.

"Did you know someone paid Candace to switch the babies?" McCall asked.

"She wouldn't have done it," Audie said. "Candace didn't have it in her."

McCall tried to tell if Audie found that a good quality about the woman or a tragic flaw. "Did you ever meet her sister?"

Audie seemed surprised. "I didn't even know she had a sister."

Again, McCall wasn't sure she believed him. "Did you have anything to do with Candace's murder?"

"Her name was Katherine Landon, not Candace Porter." He smiled at her surprise. "I was in love with her. I would have married her. In fact…" His voice broke. He turned and picked up the axe.

"You must have been devastated when she was killed, then."

"I looked for her killer," he said as he picked up a log from the pile and set it down on the chopping block. His gaze locked on hers. "I even went to the sheriff and told him that I thought Pepper Winchester had done it. He laughed me out of his office."

He raised the axe and brought it down on the log. The fall air cracked as the log split in a burst of wood chips. McCall breathed in the sweet scent of the pine, studying him. "You were the one who paid to have her buried in the cemetery," she said with sudden insight. It hadn't been the local mortuary after all.

Audie didn't deny it as he continued to chop wood.

As she drove away, McCall wasn't sure what she believed. Because sure as hell her grandmother was involved.

CYRUS WASN'T SURE what kind of reception he and Kate would get at the Winchester Ranch. Clearly his grandmother knew about all the questions he and Kate had been asking in Whitehorse.

They were just leaving for the ranch when his cell phone rang. It was McCall. She filled him in on what she'd found out from talking to Audie Dennison.

"I'm trying to locate Jace Dennison," she said.

"What do you mean, trying to locate?" Cyrus asked.

"Apparently he has a job where he is out of the country a lot," she said.

"I thought I heard he was a rodeo cowboy?"

"Was. Since college he kind of fell off the radar," McCall said.

Cyrus raised a brow. "Are you talking some kind of intelligence job like with the government?"

"Quite possibly, since I can't seem to get a line on him. But Marie is apparently getting worse. The hospice people said Jace usually contacts Marie every few weeks. They've promised to let me know when he calls."

"Hospice?"

"She's dying, that's why I'm sure once he hears, he'll return to Whitehorse at once."

"So there is little chance of getting his DNA," Cyrus said. "That means—"

"Aunt Virginia," McCall said. "She needs to be told there is a chance the baby she buried isn't hers. I don't have to tell you the kind of fireworks this is about to set off."

No, Cyrus thought, thinking of his grandmother. "If Pepper is involved she'll do her damnedest to stop you from exhuming that baby's remains."

"I'm more concerned how Virginia is going to take it," McCall said. "Losing that baby…" She shook her head. "Who knows how different Virginia's life might have been. She could have actually been happy."

Cyrus was still holding out hope that his grandmother had had nothing to do with this. He didn't want to believe that Pepper Winchester could be that heartless, that cold and calculating, and yet he suspected when it came to manipulating her family, the woman was capable of anything.

"We're headed for the ranch now," Cyrus said and heard a phone ring in the background.

"I'll meet you there," McCall said but she sounded distracted. "Cyrus? It doesn't look like I'm going to make it to dinner. We just got a call. Roberta Warren was found dead at her home."

Chapter Thirteen

As she and Cyrus drove out to the Winchester Ranch through the rolling prairie, Kate felt a sense of calm she hadn't expected. She and Cyrus had been so upset to hear about Roberta Warren. Cyrus had quizzed McCall, but she hadn't had any more information.

Now, Kate realized the reason for her sense of calm was this land. The wide-openness, the grass pale yellow against the darker brush that lined the coulees and the Little Rockies an even darker smudge of color against the horizon. The land was washed with a rich patina that shone in the sunlight.

A chinook had blown in this morning, quickly melting last night's snowfall. The way temperatures changed up in this part of the world still amazed her.

"Wait until winter," she'd been told. "One minute it will be thirty below zero, the next it will be thirty above."

Her life felt like the wild Montana weather, she thought, glancing over at Cyrus. She hadn't known what to expect this morning when she'd woken up in his arms after their lovemaking and middle-of-the-night hot chocolate.

She'd half expected him to pull away, but he hadn't. He seemed to have quit fighting this chemistry between them, this act of fate that had brought them together. But she didn't kid herself that being lovers was anything other than temporary. She knew he had to go back to his life in Denver and she to hers here in Whitehorse.

After breakfast they'd gone over to the cemetery and found her aunt's grave. She would have the headstone changed, but she had no intention of moving her aunt. As they were leaving, Kate noticed there was an empty plot next to her aunt's. Her heart had stopped for a moment as she realized that was where her mother should have been.

"Are you all right?" Cyrus asked as he slowed the pickup.

She nodded as she saw the wooden arch that read *Winchester Ranch*. She was finally going to meet Pepper Winchester. She didn't know what to expect and she had a feeling Cyrus was just as uneasy about this dinner.

It was impossible for her to imagine a mother who could let her daughter believe that her baby had died because the father of the baby was from a family she hated.

But then again, Pepper might be worse than a domineering, controlling mother. She could be a murderer.

Cyrus turned the pickup under the arch. A quarter mile down the narrow road, she spotted the lodge. It was a sprawling log structure that she realized resembled the Old Faithful Lodge in Yellowstone Park.

She'd heard about the place with its several wings and numerous levels, but she hadn't been quite prepared for this. Cyrus had said his brother told him that the inside had all the original furnishings when he'd left here twenty-seven years ago.

Kate just hoped they were all still there. She itched to see what was inside. If it really hadn't been touched for years.

For just a moment in her enthusiasm as a collector of furnishings from the past, she forgot why they were here. Instantly she sobered at the thought. She was about to meet Cyrus's grandmother and aunt Virginia.

"Pepper and Virginia are the most bitter, unhappy women I know," he said as he drove toward the lodge. "The only meaner woman I know is my grandmother's housekeeper, Enid.

Now all three of them are living here." He shook his head as if unable to imagine that.

"Maybe they have good reason to be the way they are, at least in Virginia's case," she said.

"Maybe."

He parked out front. As they got out of the pickup, an old dog growled but didn't get up from the shade of what appeared to be a large log garage.

The front door opened. A tall woman appeared.

"Grandmother," Cyrus said under his breath.

Pepper Winchester was an intimidating figure in her black clothing. Her hair was plaited in a long braid of salt and pepper. Kate could see the Winchester resemblance in her dark eyes. She had once been a beauty. No wonder she'd produced such beautiful grandchildren.

"Cyrus," his grandmother said. "I am so glad you're better." She sounded sincere.

"You might change your mind about that," he said. "We need to talk."

"After dinner," she said. "Whatever it is we have to say to each other shouldn't spoil our appetites. Then again, with Enid's cooking…" She turned her attention to Kate. "This must be your…friend. Kate Landon."

"You are well-informed," Cyrus said.

Pepper took Kate's hand in both of hers.

"Please come in," she said, not looking the least bit worried about what Cyrus wanted to talk to her about.

"I understand you have a charming shop in town," Pepper said as they entered the house.

"Thank you." Kate was surprised by the woman's warmth and her relaxed demeanor. Kate had expected her to be cold and uncaring. Even Cyrus seemed a little off-balance by his grandmother's warm welcome.

Pepper, using her cane, led them inside. "Let's go on down to the dining room. Virginia, as usual, is champing at the bit to eat and Enid gets so perturbed if dinner is a minute late. We can visit before she serves. Do you drink wine, Kate?"

"On occasion."

"Well, I'd say this was an occasion, wouldn't you?" Pepper said cheerfully. "It isn't every day that my grandson comes out of a coma and returns to the ranch."

Just as Pepper had said, Virginia was waiting in the dining room. She turned, a glass of wine in her hand, her expression softening a little at the sight of them. Kate saw at once the strong resemblance to Pepper.

But where Pepper could seem warm and charming, Kate sensed Virginia could not. Somewhere in her early fifties, she could have passed for a woman much older. Her face had deep frown lines. She looked like a woman who'd had a hard life. Kate's heart went out to her, knowing what she'd been through—and might have to face again if they were right about the babies being switched.

"Please sit down," Pepper said.

A skinny, elderly woman with wiry gray hair and a scowl appeared.

"Enid, why don't you get us another bottle of wine," Pepper said.

The woman shot her employer a sour look, but did as she was told.

Kate's head was still spinning at all the wonderful Western antiques in every room they'd passed on the way to the dining room. The dining room was no exception.

"You like what you see?" Pepper asked, smiling.

"Your home is beautifully furnished, so true to the era," Kate said, then realized that might not have sounded like a compliment. "I'm sorry."

Pepper waved her apology away as she handed her a glass of wine, then one to her grandson. For a moment the older woman's gaze seemed to study Cyrus. "I was never able to tell you and your brother apart."

"You never tried," Virginia said and downed her wine.

Her mother merely smiled. "My daughter doesn't approve of me. But then again, few members of my family do. Please, let's sit down. Virginia is much more forgiving after she's eaten."

Kate thought this evening might prove to be the exception to the rule.

The food was ghastly, the conversation stilted and the tension so thick it would have taken an axe to cut it. Pepper looked disappointed. Clearly she'd hoped it would be more enjoyable. Kate almost felt sorry for her.

Virginia was somewhat more agreeable after dinner, although obviously tipsy after all the wine she'd consumed.

"Kate and Cyrus want to have a word with me," Pepper said to Virginia after dinner. "I believe we will go down to the parlor. It is the warmest room in the house. Perhaps you'd like to join us later, Virginia."

She took the snub by snatching up the last of the second bottle of wine and stalked out of the dining room.

CYRUS CLOSED THE DOOR behind him once he, Kate and Pepper were all in the parlor. He remembered from when he was a boy what a horrible eavesdropper Enid had been. According to his brother, she'd only gotten worse.

A small fire burned in the grate. Pepper waved Kate into one of the leather chairs. Cyrus declined the other one, going to sit on the hearth as his grandmother lowered herself into the chair, her cane leaning against the chair's arm.

Pepper looked to Cyrus expectantly. "Don't be shy. You never have been, but may I ask you something first? I'm sure your brother, Cordell, already told you what I asked him."

"About the third-floor room and what we might have seen that day," Cyrus said, expecting this was the main reason they'd been invited to dinner. "I'm sure he told you I didn't see anything. He would have known."

His grandmother nodded. "But you weren't alone up there." Before he could answer, she said, "I know Jack was there, but I want to know about the other children there that day."

Cordell had already warned him that their grandmother knew they hadn't been alone, something about some party hats she'd found in the room. The third-floor room had been off-limits. It had been used as punishment when his father was a child.

"What did Jack and Cordell tell you?" he asked.

Pepper made a disgruntled sound. "I already

have my suspicions, but I want to hear it from you, Cyrus. Of the bunch, I trust you to tell me the truth."

It had been twenty-seven years. They'd all kept the secret because they'd known better than to be in that room. They also knew better than to allow anyone else in there, especially anyone from the McCormick Ranch.

But now he realized that all of the pieces of this puzzle seemed to fit together. He suddenly understood a lot more about the past.

"The McCormick girls were with us."

"They used to sneak over from their ranch all the time," Cyrus said. "I thought it was because they saw it as an adventure, knowing what would happen if they got caught. I used to wonder why they always left little things behind, hair ribbons and barrettes, paper dolls and grape bubble gum. But now I know that they came over here to taunt you and Virginia."

Pepper sighed. He'd expected her to lie or at least argue that he was wrong. She did neither. "So you know about Virginia and Jordan and the baby."

"You must have been incensed when you found out."

His grandmother smiled at that. "I could have killed Virginia."

"Instead you made sure her baby died by

paying to have her baby switched with Marie Dennison's."

Pepper met his gaze and slowly shook her head. "Is that what you think I did?"

"Someone paid Candace Porter five thousand dollars to switch the babies, then killed her."

"Oh, so now you think I not only let Virginia believe her baby had died, I also killed someone?" Pepper asked.

"You have to admit, you don't have the best record when it comes to people dying around you," he pointed out, referring to her husband, Call, who'd allegedly ridden off on horseback one day, never to return.

Pepper turned to stare into the fire. Cyrus wondered if she was contemplating burning in hell. "I have done a lot of things in my life that I'm ashamed of, but that isn't one of them."

"That doesn't answer the question," Cyrus said. "I'm sure it was justified in your warped mind. McCall is going to be paying you an official visit soon. She is getting proof that the babies were switched. Once she traces that money back to you…" He shook his head.

"Candace Porter was my aunt," Kate said. "My mother was visiting her. I'm not sure what happened to her, but we believe whoever killed Candace Porter and my mother did it to cover up the crime."

Pepper turned to meet her gaze, held it for a moment, then looked away. "I'm sorry for your loss, but I didn't kill anyone and I'm sorry, but I know nothing about your mother."

"I hope not, for your sake and your family's," Kate said quietly.

"Virginia needs to be told that Jace Dennison could be her son," Cyrus said.

His grandmother slowly turned to look at him. Her eyes were dark as caverns. "Did you ever consider that Virginia might have been the one who paid the nurse to switch the babies? Jordan McCormick dropped her like a hot piece of pipe when she told him she was pregnant. He never would have married Virginia and she knew it. Her baby dying let her save face."

"I BELIEVE HER," Kate said as they walked out to his truck. This time the dog, an old blue heeler, didn't even lift his head.

Cyrus glanced over at Kate as if she'd lost her mind. "My grandmother is guilty as hell."

"Probably. But I don't believe she had anyone killed. If she had the babies switched, it was for her daughter."

Cyrus slid behind the wheel, slammed his palm against the steering wheel and swore before reaching for the key in the ignition where he'd left it.

Kate looked up to see his grandmother

standing in the doorway. She was leaning on her cane, looking all of her seventy-two years.

"Her number was in Katherine's address book," Cyrus reminded Kate. "Don't let her frailty fool you. My grandmother has always been a force to be reckoned with." He shoved his hat back and started the pickup.

Kate noticed that Pepper was still standing in the doorway watching them leave, an expression of terrible sadness on her face. "I feel sorry for her."

Cyrus swore as he looked over at her. "Don't. I have a feeling she is finally going to get what she deserves."

"She lost her husband and youngest son, Trace?" Kate asked. "I can't imagine what it must be like to lose the man you love, let alone a child."

"Believe me, she didn't miss my grandfather. I doubt she ever loved him. As for Trace, well, him she idolized, but in the end she turned him against her, too. Trace was McCall's father. My grandmother did everything she could to break up Trace's marriage to McCall's mother, Ruby."

"Is that what happened to your father's marriage to your mother?" Kate asked quietly.

"No woman was ever good enough for Pepper's sons. Or man for her daughter. Now my grandmother is obsessed with finding out if someone in the family was a co-conspirator in Trace's death. That's why she was asking about the third-floor room."

Kate listened as he explained this room Call Winchester had used to punish his children. "It sounds horrible. Your grandmother believes one of you saw Trace's murder?"

"Or at least who else was involved. I have to admit, it is strange that Trace was killed within sight of the ranch. You see now what a screwed-up family I have?"

"Is that why you were afraid of getting involved with me?"

Cyrus shot her a look, then turned quickly back to his driving. "It doesn't matter my reasons. I *am* involved." He didn't sound happy about it.

"So your grandmother locked herself away in that ranch lodge for the past twenty-seven years." She feared Cyrus had locked himself away, at least emotionally, as well. As they drove under the Winchester Ranch sign, Kate realized something.

"Your grandmother wasn't the only one who would have been unhappy about Virginia and Jordan McCormick," she said. "If the rumor was true about Pepper and Hunt McCormick…"

Cyrus swore. "Joanna McCormick hates my

grandmother with a passion, so I would imagine there is something to the rumors about Pepper and Hunt."

"So what is this Joanna McCormick like?" she asked.

He hit the brakes, surprising her. "The McCormick Ranch is just back down the road. I say we pay her a visit."

CYRUS HATED that his visit to his grandmother had upset him more than he wanted to admit. Being back on the ranch had brought back so many memories. Good memories of when they'd all been a family.

"You never mention your mother," Kate said as if reading his mind.

He chuckled. "That's because she left when I was little. She wasn't strong enough to stand up to my grandmother, so she hit the road. I've heard she remarried and has four sons."

"I'm sorry." She squeezed his arm and let go.

He was sorry to lose her touch. When he glanced over at her, she had tears in her eyes. She quickly wiped at them. "Hey, it wasn't all bad. I was just thinking of all the great memories I had at the ranch. It was a wonderful place to grow up. Cordell and I learned to ride when we were two. We used to ride every day. We literally had the run of the ranch by the time we were seven."

"But then you were exiled," she said. "It's so sad. You have this big family and yet…"

"There's the McCormick Ranch," he said, as if needing to change the subject. "You up to this?"

She nodded. "Does Jordan still live here?"

"He was killed in a hay-baling accident about a year after Virginia gave birth."

Kate shot him a shocked look. "How horrible."

Cyrus nodded. "Joanna has two daughters, both much younger than Jordan. I haven't seen them for the past twenty-seven years and have no idea what happened to them."

As he turned into the McCormick Ranch, he thought about the bad blood between the two families and wondered what kind of reception they would get.

He also wondered what his grandmother would do with the information he'd given her about the two McCormick girls being in the third-floor room the day Trace Winchester was murdered within sight of the ranch.

That day he and his brother had had a small pair of binoculars they'd been arguing over. The last thing he remembered was Cordell letting the girls look through them. They had looked out toward the distant ridge.

What if one of them had seen the murder?

But if one of them had, why wouldn't they have said something—especially if they'd seen more than one Winchester on that ridge that day?

As CYRUS DROVE into the McCormick Ranch, Kate saw a man shoeing a horse over by an old barn. He looked up, watching them drive by.

She looked away from his intense gaze, suspecting they weren't going to get a warm welcome anywhere on this ranch.

Cyrus parked in front of the large ranch house. As Kate got out, she looked back toward the old barn. The man was still watching her and Cyrus with interest.

"Looks like everyone is over by the corral," Cyrus said and they walked over to see what was going on.

Kate knew at once that the older woman sitting on the corral fence was Joanna McCormick. At sixty-eight, Joanna was a tall, athletic-looking woman with short brown hair and a weathered face that told of many hours spent outdoors.

She was watching intently as a trainer worked with a horse in the ring. Several cowboys sat a little farther down the fence, also watching.

Kate had heard that Joanna McCormick was known for the quarter horses she raised. Cyrus said he'd seen her once years ago at a quarter-horse sale outside of Laramie, Wyoming, on a ranch where his father had been working at the time.

Her husband, Hunt, had been with her. Cyrus had described Hunt as a large, gentle-looking man with a kind face. Not handsome like Call Winchester had been. Cyrus had wondered at the time what his grandmother had seen in Hunt. And, if it was true that his grandmother had had an affair with him, why Hunt hadn't left his tightly wound, brittle wife for Pepper.

Joanna gave them only a glance from under her Western straw hat as they joined her on the corral fence. "Do I know you?" she said without looking at them.

"I'm Cyrus Winchester." Her brows shot up as she turned to give him a hard look. "And this is Kate Landon."

"What do you want?" Joanna said, turning back to what was going on in the corral.

"We need to talk to you about Jordan and Virginia," Cyrus said.

The older woman acted as if she hadn't heard him as she called to the trainer to keep the horse's head up.

"If you prefer to talk to the sheriff…" Cyrus said.

"My son is dead and I could give a damn about Virginia Winchester," Joanna replied. "So I can't imagine why the sheriff would want to talk to me."

"So you didn't pay Candace Porter to switch the babies so it appeared Virginia's had died?" Cyrus asked.

The cowboys down the fence weren't looking in their direction, but they were clearly listening.

Joanna McCormick swung her legs over and dropped off the corral fence, her face crimson with anger. "How dare you—"

"Candace Porter was my aunt," Kate said, keeping her voice low. "The other woman who disappeared at the same time was my mother. We believe whoever paid to have those babies switched killed both women to keep the secret that Jace Dennison is really your grandson."

Without a word, Joanna started for the house. Cyrus shot Kate a what-the-hell look and they followed her.

The McCormick ranch house was a sprawling two-story. Like the Winchester Ranch, it had many of the same amenities, including the western décor, Native American rugs and antler lamps and fixtures. A huge wagon wheel hung down from the ceiling in the massive living room, lights glittering from it.

A fire in the massive fireplace had died to only glowing embers.

Joanna McCormick walked to it, picked up the poker and stabbed angrily at the coals. "Isn't it enough that your grandmother tried to take my husband?" she demanded, turning to glare at them. "Now you want to try to take another woman's son?"

"You don't seem all that surprised," Cyrus said. "I think you knew all about the baby switch."

"I know nothing of the kind," she snapped. "Why would I let someone else raise my grandson?"

"Because you couldn't bear the alternative. I think you were afraid Jordan would marry Virginia."

"He would never have married her."

"Was that his idea or yours?" Cyrus asked.

"I told him that if he married her, he was off the ranch. That was all I had to do."

"Didn't you care that Virginia's baby was your flesh and blood?" Kate asked.

"Was it?" Joanna asked pointedly. "Even Jordan wasn't sure of that."

Cyrus laughed. "You remind me so much of my grandmother. You know, I wouldn't put it past the two of you to have come up with the baby switch together. You both had motive for switching the babies. Coming up with the five thousand dollars to pay off the nurse wouldn't have been that hard, even though that was a lot of money thirty years ago. You could have split it. Would be easier to cover up."

Joanna looked at him, aghast. "Your grandmother and I? We can't be in the same room together."

"Unless you had a common goal. My grandmother wasn't about to let your son marry into the Winchester family."

Joanna raised a brow at that. "Why? *She* tried to marry into the McCormick family."

"That was years ago," he pointed out.

"I have a good memory," she said. "Do you really believe Jace would have been better off being raised by Virginia?"

"You stole her baby and any chance she might have had for happiness with your son," Cyrus said. "So I guess we'll never know how different she might be today."

Kate knew Cyrus was winging it, hoping for a reaction, but Joanna McCormick, other than being furious, wasn't giving him much.

"The only thing I'm not sure about is which one of you killed Candace Porter and her sister, who was in town because she knew about the switch," Cyrus continued. "It's a toss-up which of you is more cold-blooded."

"I've heard enough," Joanna said. "If you had any evidence, the sheriff would be here, not you two. Now get out. If you don't leave I am going to call the sheriff."

"You won't have to bother calling Sheriff McCall Winchester," Cyrus said. "She'll be paying you a visit soon enough."

Joanna made an angry sound. "Too many damn Winchesters around here."

"More Winchesters than you want to admit," he said.

Some of the steel seemed to leave Joanna's spine. "What is the point of ruining Jace Dennison's life if somehow the babies did get switched? I watched him grow up, saw him at every rodeo. He's a fine young man and Marie is a wonderful mother. Are you really going to take that away from them when you aren't even certain the babies were switched?"

She looked to Kate as if hoping to find sympathy with her. "Maybe your aunt getting killed had nothing to do with either of the babies."

"Or are you worried about Jace Dennison?" Cyrus asked. "Or what's going to happen to you and the McCormick Ranch when you go to prison for murder? Maybe my grandmother will come after your husband again."

"Get out!" Joanna screeched.

Cyrus turned to leave, Kate leading the way.

"If I ever see you on my land again, I'll shoot first and ask questions later," Joanna McCormick yelled after them. Behind them they heard something break. Neither looked back.

But as they were leaving, Kate saw the man she'd seen watching them earlier. He was standing just outside and she got the impression he'd been listening to their conversation.

As Cyrus slid behind the wheel, she asked, "Who is that man?"

"What man?" he asked as he started the pickup.

"The one standing by the side of the house," Kate said. "He was watching us earlier and I think he was eavesdropping on our conversation with Joanna McCormick."

Cyrus glanced up, but when Kate followed his gaze, the man was gone.

Chapter Fourteen

"Boy, have you been stirring the pot," McCall said when she got Cyrus on his cell the next morning. "Joanna McCormick called. She is hotter than a pistol and it sounds like with good reason."

"I know I probably shouldn't have gone by there. It was a spur-of-the-moment decision," Cyrus said.

"She said you accused her of baby switching and murder and taunted her with our grandmother coming after her husband—once Joanna was behind bars." McCall laughed. "Tell me you didn't."

"I couldn't help it. Damn, she is just like Pepper. Only I swear I think she's meaner," he said.

"She wants me to arrest you for everything from trespassing to slander. I calmed her down a little. She did make it clear that if I run for sheriff again, she won't vote for me. As if she did this time."

"Sorry about that."

"Yeah, that was a real heartbreaker."

"I wouldn't be surprised if she paid to have the babies switched. As for the murder or possible murder...I don't know. She's mean enough."

"Cyrus, I didn't call you just about Joanna," McCall said, her tone suddenly serious.

He knew at once. "Roberta."

"We found a suicide note. She confessed to paying Candace Porter to switch the babies. She also confessed to killing Candace when she saw her switch the babies back."

Cyrus shot Kate a look. Moments earlier they'd been sitting at the kitchen table having cinnamon rolls and coffee. Kate had stopped what she'd been doing and was now staring at him.

"She confessed to killing Kate's mother, as well."

He was trying to get his mind around this. He'd known Roberta was involved but he hadn't expected this. "How did she kill herself?"

"Pills."

"Did she say anything else?" he asked.

"No. The confession was handwritten, the writing deteriorating pretty quickly as the pills must have taken effect."

So they might never know what she'd done with Kate's mother's body.

"Would you like me to tell Kate?" McCall asked.

"No, I'll do it." He hung up and looked at Kate. Before he could say anything, she stepped into his arms.

KATE FELT AS IF she was in shock. Roberta Warren had confessed? She'd known the hospital administrator was involved, but she'd suspected the person who'd paid her aunt to switch the babies would be Pepper Winchester or Joanna McCormick or Audie Dennison.

She'd thought there would be more.

"I'm sorry," Cyrus said. "That's all Roberta said in the suicide note."

Kate knew she should have been relieved. She'd been right about her aunt changing her mind and switching the babies back. She'd also been right that whoever had killed her aunt had also killed her mother.

She even knew why Roberta had done it.

Cyrus had said he thought a woman had cut the cable in the basement because it had taken her several tries. The crying baby doll was also something a woman was more likely to use as a threat, rather than a man.

It all added up.

So why didn't she feel some relief at knowing the truth? Instead, she just felt empty inside. She was disappointed that she wasn't going to get to bury her mother beside Katherine in the cemetery. But did she really want to know what Roberta had done to her?

She looked at Cyrus and felt the full extent of this news. It was more than an end to their search. Cyrus would be going back to Denver now. There would be no reason for him to stay any longer. The threat was over.

"Do you want me to make some hot chocolate?" Cyrus asked.

She smiled, her eyes filling with tears at his kindness, but she shook her head. Not even hot chocolate with marshmallows would work this time.

"McCall is tracing Roberta's bank statements to see if she can find the five thousand dollars," Cyrus was saying.

It took her a moment before she shot him a look of surprise. "If Roberta confessed..."

"McCall is just covering all the bases." He hesitated. "Kate, maybe you should cancel the haunted house."

"Why?" she asked studying him intently. "You don't think she acted alone?"

"Until McCall can verify Roberta's story, I would just feel better—"

"No." They'd both put their lives on hold during all this. Cyrus especially. "As far as I'm concerned, it's over. There really isn't any reason you need to—"

"I'm staying to help with the haunted house," he said, almost seeming hurt that she would try to get him to leave sooner.

A LINE HAD ALREADY formed outside Second Hand Kate's before Kate signaled for Cyrus to open the door. All the volunteers were in place. Kate couldn't have been happier with the results.

She'd gone around making last-minute changes, knowing she was only making them to keep her mind off everything that had happened. She'd also been avoiding Cyrus. He'd worked tirelessly all afternoon in the basement, changing all the locks, not only on the doors, but also the windows.

If she hadn't known he would be leaving, his effort to make her safe was a sure sign.

There was an air of excitement as the door opened and she got her first glimpse of the children and their parents pouring in. Kate told herself that Whitehorse was her home. She could handle whatever life threw at her after this.

No regrets, she thought as she took her place at the exit door. Jasmine had sewn her a devil costume. It was huge and allowed her to step into it, disappearing in the darkness by the door until it was time to give everyone one last fright.

No, she would never regret this time spent with Cyrus. Eventually she would get over him, she told herself, even though she feared she was lying.

She wondered where Cyrus was and half feared that he might have already left. He'd told her he hated goodbyes because of all the places he'd had to leave due to his father's work when he was growing up.

Maybe it would be easier if, when the haunted house closed its doors at 10:00 p.m., she would find him gone. The thought broke her heart. She couldn't imagine never seeing him again.

She brushed at the sudden tears that welled in her eyes. She could hear someone moving quickly through the maze and got ready to play her part.

CYRUS HAD TRIED to station himself where he could see Kate, but the moment she stepped back into the huge devil costume, she disappeared into the darkness from sight. The basement had quickly filled with screams of terror and excitement. It echoed through the cavernous room.

Kate and her friends had done a wonderful job. He'd been amazed how many people had been waiting outside the door and since he'd taken his position, the line had not stopped for a minute.

Kate must be so proud.

Just the thought of her tore at his heart. Maybe it would have been easier on both of them if he'd left this morning. After her successful haunted house, she would have her friends and all the volunteers to celebrate with.

He'd originally planned to leave in the morning, but he realized now that leaving tonight would be better. Kate knew he hated goodbyes. She'd understand.

The roar of the basement increased. He tried to see Kate in the darkness of the devil's cape by the back door. There was only the faint exit light glowing on the wall nearby, but every once in a while the cape moved.

He tried to relax. McCall had called earlier to tell him that they'd gotten a fingerprint off the batteries from the doll he and Kate had found in the shop crib. The print had matched Roberta's.

Cyrus still believed that someone had come up with the money to pay Candace Porter, aka Katherine Landon, to switch the babies. He was sure it had been either his grandmother or Joanna McCormick or both.

Those suspicions were confirmed when McCall called to tell him that she had found in Roberta's files that she'd made a deposit to her account on Dec. 17, 1980 for ten thousand dollars. She'd made a withdrawal for five thousand Dec. 19, 1980.

Roberta Warren must have been the go-between. Her neck must have been on the line to make sure the nurse did as she was told.

They wouldn't know if the babies had actually been switched until McCall located Jace Dennison. McCall had told him that she was having trouble getting Virginia's baby's body exhumed. Not only Pepper and Joanna were fighting it, but Virginia, as well.

Was it possible Virginia had been the one to pay to have the babies switched?

He tried to put it out of his mind. McCall was still investigating. But he had to let it go. All he cared about was that now Kate should be safe.

The devil costume hadn't moved for some time, he realized with a start. Nor had he heard anyone shriek as they exited the building for he wasn't sure how long.

He swung down from his perch and raced along the back of the horror exhibits to the exit, telling himself she was fine. The killer was dead. He had no reason to worry about her.

As he swung around the corner, he saw at once that the huge cape hung empty. Even then, he told himself she must have just stepped out of it for a moment.

Then he saw the note pinned to the fabric.

He snatched it off and stepped out of the way of the costumed revelers. He read the scrawled letters.

I have Kate. If you ever want to see her alive again come to the old hospital alone. We will be waiting.

"Cyrus?"

He jumped at the sound of Jasmine's voice. Hastily, he stuffed the note into his pocket as he turned to face her.

"Is everything all right?" she asked.

He knew he must have looked like hell. "I need you to do something for me," he said, surprised how calm he sounded. "Can you make sure everyone gets out of here and lock up? I've sent Kate to a motel. She wasn't feeling well. I'm going to go check on her now."

If Kate's friend suspected anything, she didn't let on. A part of him wanted to tell her, wanted to tell her to call the sheriff. He knew he might need backup in case things went to hell tonight, but he couldn't take the chance that if he didn't go alone, it would get Kate killed.

He left by the side door and ran the five blocks to the old hospital. It was pitch-black beside the building. He stood for a moment getting his bearings.

The inside of the building was dark, the windowpanes like blank eyes staring out. He couldn't see if someone was watching him. Or waiting just beyond the glass.

The front door was still chained and padlocked. Cyrus walked around the building to a side door. Also locked. At the back door, he slowed as he saw someone had left it ajar for him.

Away from a window, he reached into his shoulder holster and drew out his weapon. A sliver of fear embedded itself beneath his skin. He had no idea what he was going to find once he stepped inside.

All he could think about was getting to Kate. If whoever took her hurt her...

Cyrus moved to the door, listening, but heard no sound coming from inside the building.

Carefully, he eased the door open, staying to one side, then slipped into the darkness. It took a moment for his eyes to adjust before he could see a faint light coming from down the hall.

He started toward it, his boot heels echoing softly as he approached.

When he reached the corner, he saw where the light was coming from, but then again, he'd already known, hadn't he?

The light was coming from the open door of the nursery.

Chapter Fifteen

McCall had expected her cousin to go back to Denver once he'd heard about Roberta Warren's confession.

Even though he hadn't said anything, she'd bet he was as suspicious as she was. McCall didn't like it when everything got tied up too neatly. It made her cautious. That was one reason she was determined to get all the evidence together as quickly as possible.

That meant verifying everything in Roberta's confession. McCall had already contacted the president of the bank. She was meeting him there after discovering a safe-deposit box key among Roberta's possessions.

At her knock, he opened the door and led her into the safe-deposit room. Using her key and he using the bank's, she opened the box and carried it to a table.

McCall dumped the contents of the safe-deposit box on the table and began to go through it. She hadn't found anything at Roberta's death scene to indicate it had been anything but a suicide. Of course, McCall had been suspicious nonetheless. If Roberta really had been responsible for everything, then this case was over, all the missing details lost forever.

But what bothered McCall was Roberta's motive. Money? What other motive could she have had?

In her suicide note, Roberta said she'd found out that Candace was really Katherine Landon and had lied about being a registered nurse. So Roberta said she'd blackmailed her into switching the babies because Virginia Winchester had no business raising a baby and Marie Dennison deserved a child. Roberta said she'd known that Marie's baby had a weak heart.

There'd been no mention of the five grand she'd paid Candace/Katherine in the suicide note. That seemed odd to McCall.

The contents of the safe-deposit box included a stack of stocks and bonds, a large amount of cash, Roberta's husband's birth and death certificates and her own birth certificate and an envelope marked *In case of death*.

Carefully McCall opened the envelope and began to read, her heart pounding as she read Roberta Warren's *real* confession. The woman had definitely known too much.

"I'm going to need backup, two units, stat," the sheriff said, getting on the phone.

KATE STARED AT THE GUN, then at the masked man pointing it at her.

He'd appeared before the rest of the crowd had reached her, wearing a hideous monster mask. The moment Kate had seen him with the gun, she'd screamed, but the sound had been lost in the ruckus of the haunted-house revelers.

He'd grabbed her arm and shoved the barrel of the gun into her ribs. "Give me any trouble and I will kill you right here."

She'd believed him as he'd handed her a mask that covered not only her face but her hair.

"Put that on," he'd ordered, then he'd forced her at gunpoint out the side door to where he'd parked his pickup right outside her shop in the alley. Then he drove her to the old hospital.

Now she sat on the floor, her back against the wall, watching him pace. He kept looking at his watch, giving her the impression he was expecting someone. There was something about him that almost seemed familiar, but with that horrible mask covering everything but his eyes and a little slit of mouth, she couldn't place him.

"Who are we waiting for?" she asked, but like the other questions she'd asked him, he hadn't bothered to answer.

So, she sat and listened, waiting, her heart in her throat, afraid she knew exactly who they were waiting for.

As CYRUS WALKED down the hallway toward the nursery, he thought of the dream that had started all of this. It had brought him to Whitehorse, to Kate. He knew Kate had been in danger since the moment she'd set foot in this town, but it didn't make it any easier. His dream and him showing up had only put her in more jeopardy.

For days he'd been telling himself he had to get back to Denver, back to the life he and Cordell had made for themselves.

It had been fear. He'd seen his twin go through a horrible marriage and an even worse divorce. His own father had been forced to raise his sons alone because he'd married the wrong woman.

Cyrus hadn't realized just how afraid he was of falling in love until Kate. Love. He loved her. He tried to think of the exact moment it had happened and instead saw a series of moments culminating in him falling head over heels for her.

What was he so afraid of? Marriage to Kate?

Or the fear that somehow marriage would ruin what they had?

But now that he might lose Kate…

He paused to listen. This old hospital seemed even creepier tonight, although this wouldn't be the first time a killer had moved through these halls. He could almost feel the ghosts of those who had walked these halls before him. Kate's aunt, for one. And probably her sister, who had come here to find out what had happened to Katherine.

Who else? he wondered as he neared the nursery. Who was waiting for him?

He thought he could smell the person's anxiety, a mixture of fear and anger and regret. But it was thoughts of Kate that had his heart pounding. She had to be all right.

He stopped just before he reached the nursery. He knew that the killer had heard him approaching. He had to know if Kate was okay. "Kate?"

"Cyrus?" He heard both relief and fear in her voice. "Cyrus, don't—"

"Shut up," he heard someone order in a hoarse whisper. "We're waiting for you," said the muffled voice.

Cyrus stepped around the corner and into the old hospital nursery, just as he had that night in his dream.

Only this time he knew the woman on the floor.

"SO YOU'RE THE DREAMER," the man in the mask said as he pointed the gun in his hand at Kate's head. "Drop your weapon on the floor and kick it over to me…. Join your girlfriend."

The man wore a monster mask, his voice muffled behind it. Pale blue eyes peered out of the holes. Cyrus could smell the fear coming off the man and see his nerves showing in the way he held the gun.

"Why don't you take off the mask," Cyrus said as he moved over to where Kate was on the floor. He sensed the man was hiding behind the mask, not to conceal his identity, but to distance himself from what he was about to do.

"Sit down next to her," the man ordered, waving the gun.

"What's the point of the mask since you plan to kill us anyway?" Cyrus said. Kill us, then kill himself, would be his guess from the jumpy way the man was acting.

"I told you to sit down."

"Not until you take off the mask and tell me what the hell this is about."

"You are in no position to make demands," the man said angrily, his words losing a lot of their power, muffled as they were behind the mask.

Cyrus could see that the man was trying to prepare himself for what he was about to do. Otherwise he would have shot Cyrus the moment he came through the nursery door.

They stood glaring at each other, the gun shaking in the man's trembling hand. He was no killer, but Cyrus suspected he'd felt forced to kill before—and would again. He'd known the killer had nothing to lose. He realized with a start that was even more true of the man standing before him.

"I know who you are, Audie," Cyrus said. "Audie Dennison."

Audie started, clearly surprised that Cyrus knew who he was. With a furious curse, he ripped the mask from his face.

On the floor next to Cyrus, Kate let out a gasp. "He's the man I saw out at Joanna McCormick's ranch. He was shoeing a horse out there and eavesdropping on our conversation," Kate said as she pushed herself to her feet.

"I told you to stay down," Audie cried, waving the gun at her.

Kate didn't listen. Like Cyrus, Kate had to see that Audie was losing his control over them. She looked scared but unhurt and he couldn't have loved her more than he did at that moment.

"It's going to be all right," he wanted to tell her. But he couldn't be sure about that. "I love you," he said.

She glanced over at him and smiled, tears

welling in her eyes. "It's about time you realized that."

"Both of you," Audie ordered, looking scared that he was losing control of this situation, "sit down—"

"Not until you tell us what this is about," Cyrus interrupted. "Don't you owe us that much?"

"Owe *you?*" Audie bellowed. "Do you know how much pain you've caused my sister with your questions and your stupid dream?" His voice broke and tears filled his eyes, but Cyrus knew better than to try to take the gun away from him. At least not yet.

"What happened all those years ago?" Kate asked quietly.

Audie looked at her and Cyrus saw the man weaken. Clearly he wanted to get this over with, and yet the magnitude of what he was about to do had him hesitating.

"You did it for your sister," Kate said, her voice soft, comforting.

"Katherine told you about someone paying her five thousand dollars to switch the babies," Cyrus prodded.

"Five thousand?" Audie was shaking his head as if confused.

So she hadn't told him about the money. "You encouraged her to do it, knowing how much your sister wanted a baby, deserved one, unlike Virginia Winchester," Kate said, still speaking to him in that calm tone.

Audie's confusion seemed to clear as he locked onto her words. "That tramp Virginia had no business with a baby. She wasn't even married."

"But then Katherine changed her mind," Cyrus said. "She betrayed you."

A sadness filled the man's eyes along with a deep anger. "I loved her. I would have done anything for her. She promised. I heard her talking to her sister on the phone by the nurses' station. She'd left the cart with the medical supplies in the hallway. I didn't even realize I'd picked up the scalpel."

"You had no choice but to kill her sister, too," Cyrus said.

"You're the one who left the bracelet on my grandmother's doorstep," Kate said.

"It was a foolish, sentimental thing to do," Audie admitted. "But I couldn't throw it away and I couldn't keep it, either."

Kate began to cry softly.

"I couldn't let it come out about the babies," Audie said angrily. "Marie was so happy. Of course she was sad about Virginia's baby dying. Marie is that kind of woman. I owed her. I had to do whatever it took to make her happy."

"And you did," Cyrus said. "Roberta Warren must have known it was you. Was she threatening you? Is that why you had to stop her?"

Audie blinked. "That old hag at the hospital?"

Cyrus felt his stomach clinch. Audie Dennison hadn't killed Roberta. Nor had he known about the five thousand dollars that had changed hands. "Whose idea was it to switch the babies? Who paid Katherine to do it?"

IT TOOK MCCALL too long to find Jasmine in the depths of the haunted house. "Where are Kate and Cyrus?"

Jasmine looked surprised and instantly worried. "Cyrus said he sent her to a motel and that he was going to join her. I thought it was odd. No way would Kate have left her haunted house before it even got started good." Her eyes widened in realization.

"You've been right here since the haunted house opened, right?" McCall said. "Who came through at the beginning?"

Jasmine frowned, clearly working to remember. She rattled off a few names of families she remembered. "Wait a minute. The first person who came in didn't even have a kid with him. I thought it was funny, but I figured he must be a volunteer Kate had recruited and he was late and that's why he rushed in the way he did."

"Jasmine, who—"

"Audie Dennison."

AUDIE FROWNED. "How would I know who paid her to switch the babies?" he demanded. "I thought she was doing it out of the goodness of her heart. I was going to marry her…" He was waving the gun again, clearly upset. "I was in love." His gaze seemed to focus on the two of them. "Like you." His voice broke.

"Audie," Cyrus said, seeing something in the man's eyes that turned his blood to ice.

"My sister Marie died tonight."

Before Cyrus could move, Audie turned the gun on himself. The loud report echoed through the nursery, a thunder of pain-ending sound.

Cyrus grabbed Kate, sheltering her from the sight as Audie Dennison dropped to the floor, his gun clattering to the worn tiles. And Cyrus found himself again standing in the old hospital nursery with a body lying in a pool of blood.

As he took Kate in his arms, he heard the sound of sirens in the distance.

Epilogue

Kate heard the racket outside the front door of the shop and hurried to see what was going on. She hadn't seen Cyrus all morning and now when she looked out, she caught a glimpse of him through the thickly falling snow.

As she opened the door, he dragged in a Christmas tree and stood it up for her inspection. "So, what do you think?" Both he and the tree were covered in fresh snow. She breathed in the scent of pine and snow.

What did she think? That she loved this man more than life.

Love had saved them. As corny as it sounded, Kate knew that the love she and Cyrus shared that moment in the old hospital nursery had saved their lives.

She'd seen the change in Audie Dennison. He'd come there to kill them. He'd killed before. She didn't doubt that he would have done anything to spare his sister. But Marie was dead and while Audie had nothing to lose, he couldn't bring himself to kill again. Not two people who anyone could see adored each other.

McCall had arrived moments after the sound of the gunshot died away. She'd come barreling in, weapon drawn, fear that she'd arrived too late in her eyes. Maybe blood *was* thicker than water, because Kate could see that McCall had true affection for her cousin. It would be nice for McCall to have family again. And Cyrus, too.

She knew how relieved he was to find out that his grandmother had had nothing to do with switching Virginia's baby with Marie's. Kate thought maybeVirginia and Pepper's relationship might have a chance to heal and that McCall's Christmas wedding could bring the entire Winchester family back together.

Cyrus was still concerned that his grandmother was up to something and anxious about the wedding. He didn't want anything to go wrong for McCall and Luke. Only time would tell, but Kate, always the optimist, thought this could be the most perfect Christmas ever for all of them.

She was looking forward to the Christmas wedding, which was now only two weeks away.

Whitehorse had been shocked when the news

had come out that Joanna McCormick had been arrested for the murder of Roberta Warren. McCall had found proof, not only in Roberta's real confession, but also in phone records, bank accounts and DNA from the scene at Roberta's house.

Faced with all the evidence, Joanna McCormick had confessed it all. She was the one who had paid Roberta ten thousand dollars to switch the babies. Joanna would have done anything to keep her son from Virginia Winchester— including letting him believe his infant son had died.

What Joanna didn't know was that Roberta used blackmail and five thousand dollars to try to coerce Katherine into making the switch.

Joanna had hired Audie to do more than shoe some of her horses. She'd paid him to try to scare off Kate, and when he'd balked, she'd taken the job into her own hands. She'd been the one to cut the cable and put the doll in the nursery. She'd had a key to the old library back when her husband, Hunt, had been on the library board.

After the shock and horror of what had happened, Kate had been filled with a deep sadness, but Cyrus had been there for her. It turned out that Roberta Warren wasn't the only one to leave a detailed true confession of her part in all this. Audie Dennison had left one as well at his house.

That confession had given Kate the greatest peace of mind. He'd told her where he'd buried her mother. She'd been able to have her mother's remains buried properly next to her aunt's at the local cemetery.

The sisters were now buried side by side, with matching headstones and inscriptions with their real names and the dates they had died. Earlier Kate had gone by the cemetery to put Christmas wreaths on her aunt's and mother's graves. It seemed fitting that they were together again.

"I know the tree is a little flat on that one side, but I thought we could put it against the wall," Cyrus said now, looking worried that she didn't like it.

She smiled, still taken aback sometimes at how lucky she'd been to have him come into her life. She liked to think her aunt and mother had had something to do with that.

"I love the tree," Kate said as she stepped toward him. "And look what I have." She held mistletoe over their heads and saw his dark eyes shimmer with love. His kiss made her toes curl and her heart pound.

But it was nothing like his proposal that night under their first Christmas tree. An odd thing happened when she said yes. She thought she heard the sound of tiny tinkling sleigh bells and glanced toward the glassed-in case where her mother's and her aunt's bracelets now rested side by side.

* * * * *

LARGER-PRINT BOOKS!

GET 2 FREE LARGER-PRINT NOVELS

PLUS 2 FREE GIFTS!

HARLEQUIN®

INTRIGUE®

Breathtaking Romantic Suspense

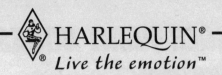

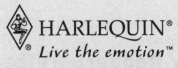

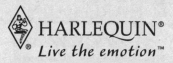

HARLEQUIN®
Presents®

**The world's bestselling romance series...
The series that brings you your favorite authors,
month after month:**

Helen Bianchin...Emma Darcy
Lynne Graham...Penny Jordan
Miranda Lee...Sandra Marton
Anne Mather...Carole Mortimer
Melanie Milburne...Michelle Reid

and many more talented authors!

Wealthy, powerful, gorgeous men...
Women who have feelings just like your own...
The stories you love, set in exotic, glamorous locations...

HARLEQUIN®
Presents®

Seduction and Passion Guaranteed!

Harlequin® Historical
Historical Romantic Adventure!

*Imagine a time of chivalrous
knights and unconventional ladies,
roguish rakes and impetuous
heiresses, rugged cowboys
and spirited frontierswomen—
these rich and vivid tales will
capture your imagination!*

*Harlequin Historical . . .
they're too good to miss!*